THOMAS TREW
AND THE HORNS OF PAN

SOPHIE MASSON

Illustrated by Ted Dewan

**Hodder
Children's
Books**

A division of Hodder Headline Limited

To Rosemary, my agent

Dear Reader,

Do you wish you could leave the ordinary world and go into an extraordinary one, full of fun and magic and adventure – and danger? You do? Well, so does Thomas Trew – and one grey London afternoon, his wish comes true!

Two amazing people come calling at his house – a dwarf called Adverse Camber and a bright little lady named Angelica Eyebright. They tell Thomas he's a Rymer and he has a destiny in their world, the world of the Hidden People.

It's a world of magic – what the Hidden People call 'pishogue'. It's a world of extraordinary places and people – the Ariels, who live in the sky; the Seafolk, who live in the ocean; the Montaynards, who live in the rocks and mountains; the Uncouthers, who live deep underground, and the Middlers who live on the surface of the earth.

But not everyone in the Hidden World is pleasant or friendly, and some of them, like the Uncouthers, are very nasty indeed . . .

In the first adventure, *Thomas Trew and the Hidden People*, Thomas and his father Gareth come to live in Owlchurch, and begin to learn what it means to be a Rymer. He learns, too, about the rivalry between homely little Owlchurch and Aspire, the glamorous village across the river. And then he falls into great danger when he stumbles into the Uncouthers' country and is brought face to face with General Legion Morningstar, their cruel leader, who has some very unpleasant plans for him!

Now Thomas is back in Owlchurch, safe and sound. Or is he? Read on!

ONE

Unicorns may be beautiful, but they're also bad-tempered. And when they're angry, things are likely to get broken, and people get hurt. So when Patch Gull, out gathering mushrooms in the woods, heard the distinctive scream of an angry unicorn, she didn't hesitate. Dumping her basket of mushrooms, she shinned up the nearest big tree and hid high in the leafy branches.

She was just in time. The unicorn galloped into the clearing an instant later, and skidded to a sudden stop. Patch peered cautiously down. It was a big white unicorn, and its blood was well up. Its big green eyes rolled wildly and its wickedly sharp horn swept from side to side as the beast swung its head this way and that, as if looking for someone. Patch kept absolutely still, hoping that it wouldn't see the tell-tale basket at the foot of the tree. The unicorn stood there a moment longer, puffing and snorting. Suddenly it went quite still. It trembled, gave a high-pitched whinny, turned, and thundered out of the clearing again. In an instant, it had vanished into the trees. In another instant, even the sound of its galloping hooves had died away.

Patch waited a minute or two after that, just to be on the safe side. Then she scrambled down, picked up her basket of mushrooms and set off home as fast as she could. You didn't often see unicorns in this part of the wood. What had happened to put it in such a state? Mind you, it didn't take much to spook the silly things!

When Patch got home, she found her twin

brother Pinch and their human friend Thomas Trew, playing cards. She was immediately jealous.

'You said you'd wait till I came back, Pinch!' she shrieked.

'No,' said Pinch, grinning. 'I only said I'd wait till the chores were finished!' He jerked a knobbly greenish thumb at a bowl in the sink. '*My* chores, that is! I chopped up all those herbs Mother said I had to do. And Thomas helped me, so it went quicker.'

Patch glared at Thomas, who blushed.

'Pinch didn't tell me you'd be back so soon. He said you'd be ages, and that you'd said it was OK if I showed him a few things first.'

Patch launched herself at Pinch, and they rolled around on the floor, kicking, scratching, biting. In the commotion, Patch completely forgot about the unicorn and its strange behaviour. By the time she and Pinch stopped fighting, made up and demanded that Thomas teach them both together, the horned

4

beast had retreated to the furthest corners
of her memory.

TWO

Thomas Trew and his father Gareth had been living in Owlchurch for quite a few weeks now. Thomas hadn't quite forgotten London, where he used to live, but he practically never thought about it. It was too much fun being in the Hidden World, like being permanently on holidays. His adventure in the dark Uncouther city of Pandemonium had left him none the worse for wear. He still thought of it occasionally, but as there'd been no more trouble from the Uncouthers, he'd stopped worrying about it.

At the moment, what he was chiefly thinking about was the magic the twins were teaching him in exchange for the card games he was showing them. It was just minor pishogue – fun magic like short-term 'thinning', or invisibility, and a basic 'long-stalker' spell, which turned ordinary shoes into seven-league boots, or seven-league sneakers, anyway.

Even this level of minor pishogue wasn't easy, and had its dangers, for a human, even a Rymer like Thomas who could move in and out of both Hidden and Obvious Worlds fairly easily. 'Thinning', for instance, could have the nasty side-effect of unbearably itchy skin rashes. They could become permanent if you didn't snap out of invisibility pretty quickly. Teaching anything more complicated to humans was forbidden, except on special licence. That was only granted to certain skilled and trusted types of enchanters and witches, who were closely supervised on short-stay visits and conferences in the Hidden World. And some things were out of bounds altogether to humans – for instance, the production of dreams.

It took Thomas time to learn the spells, but he was getting fairly good at them. The twins didn't find the card games quite as easy. Thomas forbade the use of magic, though Pinch, who hated losing, tried to cheat a number of times. He'd 'thinned' the cards once or twice, and cast a spell of energy over them another time, so that they jumped out of Thomas's hands like crickets escaping. Yet he'd still lost! But Patch didn't mind losing. She was fascinated by the cards, and by the games, such as Old Maid and Beggar My Neighbour, that Thomas taught them.

They were just about to finish a game of Go Fish when the door opened and Old Gal came in. Thomas hastily gathered the cards together and shoved them in his jeans pocket. He wasn't at all sure if the twins' mother would approve of her children being taught 'Obbo' ways. But Old Gal took no notice. She was looking more rumpled and cross than usual.

'Where's my cloak? Oh, there!' She looked at

the children. 'I have to go out on urgent business. I may be gone a little while.'

The twins were instantly alert. 'Why? What's happened, Mother?' cried Pinch.

Old Gal waved a vague hand. 'Oh, just something in the village.'

'Where are you going?' Patch said, but Old Gal had gone. The three children looked at each other.

'She looked cross,' said Pinch.

'No, anxious,' said Patch.

'I think she looked surprised,' said Thomas. 'Bewildered,' he corrected himself.

'We've got to know what's going on!' said Pinch, firmly. 'Let's go down the village and talk to Hinkypunk.'

Hinkypunk Hobthrust had the Tricks Shop. He seemed to know what was going on more than almost anyone else in the village aside from Angelica Eyebright, and she was away on one of her mysterious trips again. As were, in fact, a fair few people, such as the baker

Cumulus Zephyrus, who'd gone to visit his Ariel relatives; and Calliope Nightingale, the musician, who'd gone in search of new tunes. Morph Onery the dream-maker and Monotype Eberhardt the bookseller were in charge of the village; and both of them were rather vague. Only Hinkypunk would be sure to know all the gossip.

'Hinkypunk won't tell *us*,' said Patch, shaking her head.

'You're just scared of him,' sneered Pinch.

'No, I'm not! It's you who—'

'Somebody else might tell us,' said Thomas, hastily. 'Let's go and try, anyway.'

THREE

The village seemed quiet enough. Indeed, it seemed far *too* quiet. There wasn't the usual afternoon bustle; no Hinkypunk on his doorstep, smoking his long pipe; no owlish Monotype Eberhardt, the bookseller, tying down rebellious books in his window, especially the flighty novels that were always trying to flap their pages and escape into the world. And the lights of Morph Onery's Dream Emporium didn't seem to be on. But there was the dwarf Adverse Camber, looking with great interest at an unusual little vehicle that had been parked just outside the door of the Apple Tree Café. It was a dainty little carriage, painted white, green and silver,

and it was drawn by a pair of pretty white ponies. As they came closer, Thomas saw that some kind of crest was painted on it. He peered at it. It was a pair of curling goats' horns, shining silver on a dark green background. Above it was written 'By Appointment to His Majesty the King'.

He heard the Gull twins' quick intake of breath. Patch whispered, 'The Horns of Pan! It's a visitor from Arkadia!'

Pinch said, excitedly, 'But there haven't been visitors from Arkadia for . . . well, I can't remember *any* coming here! Mr Camber, who *is* it? It's not King Pan, is it?'

Adverse shook his head. He was walking around the carriage, tapping at it lightly now and again, bending down to touch the wheels. The ponies watched him incuriously. Their eyes were a soft blue, fringed by very long lashes.

The dwarf straightened, and looked at them. He said, 'I think I'd better go and fetch Angelica Eyebright. She'll want to meet them.' He jerked a thumb towards the café. 'Tell them in there it might take me a little while to find her, but I'll be back as quickly as I can. Tell them not to decide anything till we're back.'

'Decide what? Mr Camber, who—?'

'I've got to go.' Adverse Camber was setting off at a run towards his own vehicle, the talking car, Metallicus, that had been snoozing quietly in the sun. The children heard Metallicus' grouchy protest as the dwarf revved the engine, then the car sped off down the road that led out of the village.

The children looked at each other. What *could* have happened to make Adverse hurry like that? There was only one way to find out. With one mind, they raced up the steps to the café.

The front room of the Apple Tree Café was crowded with chattering people, all the people who were missing from the streets. From where he was standing, Thomas could just about see a stranger's blonde head, bobbing in and out amongst the familiar Owlchurch faces. These must be the visitors from Arkadia. He'd heard that Arkadia was an enchanted kingdom on the far side of the great forest, ruled over by Pan. Arkadia, one of the Hidden World's oldest kingdoms, was famous for its magic. He couldn't wait to see what Arkadians looked like. He followed the path Pinch and Patch's sharp elbows made in the crowd, and finally found himself face to face with the strangers.

There were three of them, a beautiful golden-haired woman and her two beautiful blond children. Twins by the look of them; a boy and a girl, like the Gulls, but as unlike those two ragamuffins as it was possible to be. These children were dressed in matching neat green and silver outfits; their hair was shining and softly-brushed, their eyes were as blue and long-lashed as those of the ponies. They looked like a pair of little angels on a Christmas card, thought Thomas, as he gazed at them. And their mother – for so she must be, they looked so like her – was like the angel, or the fairy, at the top of the Christmas tree.

She had eyes of that same soft blue, and her hair shimmered like spun gold. She was dressed in a flowing dress the colour of new

beech leaves. Over that she wore a transparent silver cloak that looked as though it had been spun of dew and cobwebs. On her arm glittered a carved silver bracelet and at her throat was a silver medallion. On both these was engraved the same crest as on the carriage. Surrounded by the admiring crowd, she was smiling and nodding as people spoke over each other. As he gazed at her, Thomas was seized with a strange feeling. He thought, I've seen her before – or someone rather like her. But he couldn't for the life of him think where. Perhaps it was just that she reminded him of a fairy on a Christmas tree.

He started as Patch spoke into his ear. 'I don't think she's an Arkadian. She looks more like an Ariel.' The Ariels were the gifted, graceful sky-dwellers of the Hidden World. Occasionally one might come and live on earth. The Owlchurch baker, Cumulus Zephyr, was an Ariel, for instance. 'But she's obviously *been* to Arkadia,' Patch went on, 'and she's been granted its highest honour – the Horns of Pan. It means that a person's pishogue is the very best. It means not only that the whole of the Hidden World respects you, but also that you can set up as a teacher of human witches and enchanters.'

At that moment, the woman turned her eyes to them. She ignored the Gulls and focused a dazzling smile on Thomas. 'Oh, Mr Trew,' she said, 'this must be your son, the Rymer.' Her voice was sweet, silvery, beautiful. Her eyes looked deep into Thomas's, and he felt warmth flowing into him. She smiled. 'How handsome he is! But that is not surprising, of course.'

Both Thomas and his father flushed. Gareth, it seemed, couldn't take his eyes off the beautiful Ariel. 'Oh, but you are too kind! Thomas, meet Mrs Peree. Mrs Frodite Peree. And her children, Silvan and Faunia . . . They are coming to live here. I am sure you will all be great friends.'

Thomas looked quickly back at the Gull

twins, but they had melted back into the crowd. *'Living here?'* he said.

'That's right. Mrs Peree and her children want to settle in Owlchurch, isn't that wonderful?'

Morph Onery said, eagerly, 'She is direct from great triumph in Arkadia, and is an ointment-maker of the rarest repute! She has been granted the Horns of Pan – the only such award granted in years and years. We are lucky indeed she has elected Owlchurch as her place of practice – she could have chosen anywhere at all, anywhere! It will mean our name will become famous through all of the Hidden World!'

'One in the eye for the Aspirants,' drawled Hinkypunk, raising a wry red eyebrow.

Aspire, the elegant township across the water, was Owlchurch's greatest rival, and considered itself much better than its cheerfully ramshackle neighbour.

'Oh, you mean that gleaming place across

the water,' said Frodite Peree, shuddering. 'It's all too flashy and modern for me. Why, all that metal and glass, it is so unnatural, I think, it makes me positively sick. I love dear, quiet, green little places like this. You see, my friends, I am really a very shy solitary. Give me Owlchurch's quiet woods and quiet pace any day! That's the place for real, traditional magic!'

The villagers grinned at each other, delighted by this dismissal of their snobby neighbour. Monotype Eberhardt spoke for them all when he said, heartily, 'We are most glad indeed you think so, dear Madam. It is a great honour you are choosing to live here amongst us. Our Mayor, Angelica Eyebright, is away, but I know she would like us to make you as welcome as possible.'

'Oh, that reminds me, Adverse Camber has gone to get her,' butted in Thomas. 'He asked us to tell you. And he said he'd be away for a little while, it would take him some time to find her. He said not to take any decision until he got back and . . .' He trailed off, seeing the expressions on the others' faces.

'Really, Adverse has got a hide,' huffed Morph Onery. 'While Angelica's away, it's me and Monotype who are in charge. Our decisions are as good as hers.' He glared at Thomas. 'I'm sure Angelica trusts us to make the right decisions. And I'm sure she'd want us to make a holder of the Horns of Pan very welcome indeed.'

'I'm sorry,' said Thomas, flushing, 'it's not my . . .'

Morph Onery turned away from him, and back to the Ariel, who'd been watching this with an unreadable face. 'Now, my dear Mrs Peree, we must find you the right spot for your house.'

'Oh, don't worry about that,' broke in the woman, smiling. 'I have picked out the perfect spot; a little clearing just at the edge of the woods, not far from the river.'

There was a slightly uncomfortable silence. Then Thomas burst out, 'But that's the clearing near the Gulls' house! Mrs Gull – she's not going to like that!' No wonder Old Gal looked so upset! Surely there isn't room for two ointment-makers in the village, he thought.

Gareth glared at his son. 'Thomas! Don't butt in. That's no business of yours, surely.' Morph Onery said, rather sternly, 'Your father's right, Thomas. Keep out of this. Madame Peree is holder of the Horns of Pan, granted to her in Arkadia itself, because of her great talents and skills. She outranks Old Gal by a great distance. We are fortunate she has come. Old Gal understands that. You'll see.'

'But that's not—' Thomas tried, but he got no further. His father glared at him again.

'Take Silvan and Faunia upstairs, help them get freshened up. They've had a long journey.'

Thomas looked at the children. All this time, they hadn't spoken a word, and the expression on their faces hadn't changed at all from a bland smile. Now, they turned their faces to him, but still their expression didn't change. It was beginning to give Thomas the creeps.

'Now off you go, be a good host, if you can,' snapped Gareth.

'Yes, Dad,' said Thomas, reluctantly. He took a last look around for Pinch and Patch, but they were nowhere to be seen. As he turned back to the children, he met Frodite Peree's eye. Something leapt into that soft blue of hers, something sharp and laughing. It gave him quite a turn; but it lasted only a tiny instant, so tiny that afterwards he was sure he must have imagined it. Almost straight away, the expression in her eyes was gentle and kind as ever.

FOUR

Thomas sat on his bed and listened to the sounds of splashing in the bathroom. He listened for the sound of conversation, too, but he could hear nothing. Either they weren't speaking to each other, or they were speaking so softly he couldn't hear them. He sat and fumed, wondering why the Owlchurchers were quite so eager to welcome these strangers who had turned up so unexpectedly.

OK. So they had been to Arkadia, that mystical kingdom so famous in the Hidden World. OK. So they had the Horns of Pan. OK. So that meant that Peree woman had great talent. OK. She was also beautiful, as were her children, with that ethereal beauty often possessed by the Ariels, who came from the lands in the clouds. But did that justify the fawning of Morph Onery and the others? Or the fact they seemed to be happy to push poor Old Gal out of the way? No wonder she had looked so bewildered and upset. Where had she gone? Surely she hadn't left . . .

The bathroom door opened. In a cloud of steam, the twins stepped out, holding each other's hands. They looked no different from before. But then, they'd been perfect, anyway.

They looked at Thomas. Thomas looked back. He thought he saw something like anxiety in their glance, and saw how they clutched each other's hands. A little pity welled up in him. He wondered what they thought of being here, amongst strangers.

'You OK? You want to eat something?'

They stared at him fearfully. Then they shook their heads.

'You want to have a rest?'

More shaking of heads. Thomas didn't know what to say next. How to make them feel at home, as Dad had said. 'Do you want to have a look at some of my books? Or play a game?'

In answer, they just held each other's hands more tightly, and shook their heads, staring at Thomas as if he was going to eat them up or something. Annoyed, he snapped, 'Can't you even speak? Cat got your tongue or something?'

The effect of his simple ill-temper was dramatic. The twins stared at him, then burst into loud wails. At that most unfortunate moment, the bedroom door opened, and Gareth and Frodite Peree came in. They took in the picture at once.

'Thomas! What have you done!' Gareth Trew was furious.

The twins rushed over to their mother's side. They clung to her, sobbing, occasionally darting a scared look at Thomas, as if he were a monster. Thomas felt very bad indeed. 'I'm sorry,' he said, helplessly, 'I didn't mean—'

'For goodness' sake, Thomas,' said his father, cutting him off, 'what's wrong with you today? Really, I'm surprised by your attitude.'

'But, Dad, I didn't do any—'

'I don't want to hear your excuses. That's quite enough. I expect better behaviour from you. And I want you to leave your bedroom for the children tonight. You can sleep in the spare room.'

All this time, the Peree family had not said anything, apart from the children's fading sobs. Frodite Peree, though, had a sad, disappointed expression on her face – an expression which made Thomas feel worse. Now, she said, softly, 'Mr Trew, there is really no need for a Rymer to give up his bed for my poor children. They can sleep on the floor, near the fire. It will be quite enough. Really it will.'

'Not at all,' said Gareth. His face was very red now, his eyes very bright. 'I *insist* that you give up your room, Thomas. How could you possibly leave our honoured guests to sleep on the hard floor?'

Thomas said, indignantly, 'But I never—'

His father flapped a hand at him. 'No more words, Thomas. You've done quite enough for today. Now get out of here, and let these poor children have a rest.'

'You are very kind, Mr Trew,' said Frodite Peree, gently. 'Very kind to me and my children. It balms my heart.' She looked at Thomas, and reached over to pat him on the hand. He flinched. 'I understand, my dear, how you must feel, strangers coming into your village, taking your bed. But it won't be for long. Tomorrow morning, I promise, everything will be different. I will begin to ply my humble solitary's trade, and my children will learn to become Owlchurchers. Oh, Thomas, I do so hope you and they will become good friends. My children have been so lonely.'

It was Thomas's turn to go scarlet. 'Mrs

Peree, I really didn't mean to . . . I mean, I'm quite happy for them to have my bedroom for as long as . . . I'm sorry if . . .'

'Don't worry, child,' said the woman. Her expression was soft and kind, but deep down in her eyes, something else stirred for an instant, that same puzzling, laughing expression he'd caught sight of, earlier. Then it was gone.

Unease washed through him. He stammered, 'Er, Dad, if you don't mind . . . there's something I must do . . . that I promised to help Old Gal with . . .'

'Go on, then,' said Gareth, sighing heavily. 'But be back before dark.'

FIVE

When Thomas got back to the Gull house, he found it deserted. Heart beating fast, he ran off to the river, and found Pinch and Patch there, skimming stones moodily into the water. They looked up gloomily at him. 'Oh, hello. We thought you'd stay down there, like the others.'

'She's an ointment-maker,' said Thomas, flinging himself down. 'And she wants to live near you, *right* near you.'

'Mother will be furious,' said Patch, sadly, 'but it won't do any good.'

'What do you mean?' said Thomas.

'That Peree woman's got the Horns of Pan.'

'So what?'

'So *what*, Thomas? You have to be joking.'

'It's only like a kind of royal appointment,' said Thomas, doggedly. 'It doesn't mean you'll have your head cut off if you don't help them, does it?'

Pinch and Patch looked at each other, and shook their heads. 'Thomas, you just don't understand,' said Patch, patiently. 'If anyone is granted the Horns of Pan, it means like – like they become like a great lord of magic or something. They outrank just about everyone in their field. Poor Mother – she's really good at what she does, but she's never been anywhere near the Horns of Pan. It's very rare to get them, you know, especially these days.'

'Why these days?'

Pinch shrugged. 'I don't know. I think King Pan thinks our magic is not as good as it used to be. He's a bit of a stick-in-the-mud, you know, and—'

'Pinch, you shouldn't say that,' said Patch,

sharply, glancing around, as if afraid someone else was listening.

'I will so say it! Anyway, whatever, there haven't been many Horns of Pan handed out recently. That's why everyone is so excited. Especially because she's chosen to come here after what happ—'

'Pinch!' broke in his sister, sharply. She went on, quickly, 'If you have the Horns of Pan, you see, you can not only choose to live wherever you want in the Hidden World, but even the Uncouthers have to respect it. No one – *no one* – in the Hidden World, not even General Legion Morningstar, would ever dream of hindering you, let alone hurt you.'

'In fact,' added Pinch, 'you can even go and live in the Obvious World if you want to, without permission. That crest is their passport to everything. They can demand anything they want, at any time. There's nothing anybody can do. They could even take our home, and demand we go into exile, and there's nothing we can do about it.'

'That's unfair!' shouted Thomas. 'I'd never let that happen! Or if it did, I'd go into exile with you,' he added, fiercely.

Pinch and Patch looked at each other. 'That's really nice of you,' said Patch, softly.

'It's not *nice*,' snapped Thomas. 'It's normal. I'm your friend. I'd never let anyone do that to you. If Owlchurch does that to you, then I don't want to be their Rymer any more. We can go back to London. You can come with me!'

'Wow,' said Pinch, eyes alight. Then he shook his head. 'We can't do that, Thomas. Mother would never go; and we have to stay with her. We have to help her. It wouldn't be fair, to leave her here having to face that Ariel on her own.'

'I don't like her,' said Thomas, slowly. 'And those children of hers – they look so perfect, but they're quite weird. And they got me in real trouble.' Quickly, he recounted what had happened. 'I didn't mean to be rough with them,' he finished. 'But they were getting on my nerves, just staring at me and shaking their heads like that. There's something odd about them all.'

The twins nodded gloomily.

'There's something else, too,' said Thomas. 'I thought when I first saw her that she reminded me of someone. But I can't think who.'

'How could you have seen her before, if she's an Ariel, and she's just come out of Arkadia?'

'I know. I can't have done, really. It's just a nagging feeling I get.'

'I know,' said Patch. 'There's something not quite right about them. But it's hard to put your finger on it. Anyway, it's pointless us trying to talk to the others about it. You won't find anyone else who'll agree.'

'Adverse Camber seemed rather uncertain
her.'

nd he's gone to fetch Angelica, but
d is that? It's true that Morph and

Monotype have just as much right to make decisions as she does. They're senior members of the village council. And they've made up their minds. You can see that clear as day. They love the Perees already. You saw Morph Onery's face? And Monotype's? They were staring like lovesick cows.'

'Dad too,' said Thomas, gloomily.

'Yes. They'll think we're just being jealous and rude. And besides, quite apart from anything else, they're really pleased that this is one over Aspire. You see, Angelica and Morph are holders of the Horns of Pan too, but so are Mr Tamblin and the Lady Pandora. This makes us one better than—'

She broke off. There was a procession coming their way: a whole group of Owlchurchers, marching happily up the hill towards the Gulls' cottage, escorting the Perees' carriage. Thomas and the twins looked at each other, the same foreboding in their minds. Then, as one, they raced for the cottage.

* * *

The carriage had drawn up. The Gulls flung themselves at the doorway, barring it with their bodies, arms folded.

'Pinch and Patch Gull,' came Morph Onery's stern voice, 'what do you think you're doing? This is no way to welcome guests.'

'Wait a minute,' began Pinch, defiantly. 'We don't—'

Then he gulped and stopped, for his mother had stepped out from behind the carriage. Her face was set in grim lines. 'Mother, you're back,' he stammered.

'Yes. Children, move away from the door,' she said, harshly. As Pinch and Patch and Thomas stared, she opened the door of the carriage, gave a short bow – Old Gal, who had never bowed to anyone! – and stepped aside so as to let the carriage's occupants out.

Frodite Peree and her children came out like a long-lost royal family, returning to a country that had been longing for them. The woman laid a slim, elegant hand on Old Gal's shoulder as she passed. Knowing how fiercely proud the twins' mother was, Thomas trembled – but Old Gal did nothing. He couldn't believe it. What had happened to her?

Frodite Peree faced the twins, who had fallen back from the door. 'I have only come to look at your mother's workshop,' she said, softly. 'I hope very much your mother will work for me, her goods sound of very high standard.'

Thomas and the twins stared at Old Gal, expecting her to bristle. But she didn't. Instead, she nodded, grimly, and gestured at the twins to let them pass. Reluctantly, they moved aside. Frodite Peree went in like a queen inspecting her domain, Old Gal humbly after her.

All the others crowded in after her. But Thomas and the twins stayed outside.

'I can't believe it,' whispered Thomas. 'Your mother – she's just going to accept this stranger lording it over her.'

'She has no choice,' said Patch, sadly.

'I can't believe that the other Owlchurchers think it's all right!'

'This is the Hidden World, Thomas, not your world.' They started. Hinkypunk stood behind them, his teeth bared in a knowing grin. 'That's the way things work here. Isn't that so, Gull children?'

They nodded, miserably, heads bent.

'Old Gal's been lucky,' said Hinkypunk, lightly. 'By all the rules, after what happened with your father, she shouldn't have been allowed to stay here. She was lucky Angelica's not the usual kind of Mayor. In Aspire, she wouldn't have stood a chance.'

The twins glared at Hinkypunk. Then, without a word, they turned and ran off down the hill towards the river, Thomas hurrying after them.

SIX

'Pinch and Patch, you're my friends,' Thomas said, gently, as he sat down beside them on the riverbank.

They didn't turn their heads, but mumbled, 'Sure.'

'Well, then, will you please tell me? What did Hinkypunk mean? What happened to your father? And why were people really so pleased that Frodite Peree's come to live here? Is it connected? What happened?'

'That's a lot of questions,' said Pinch, tightly. 'And they're not really your business.'

'Pinch!' Patch laid a hand on his arm. 'Don't talk to Thomas like that. He's our true friend. Remember what he said, before, about taking us to London.'

Pinch looked sulky and miserable. He threw a stone into the water with great force, but said nothing. Patch went on, in a rush, 'Yes, it's all connected. You see, Thomas, our mother was not meant to marry our father. *He is not from Owlchurch.*'

Thomas laughed. 'Is that all? What sort of crime is that? Oh, I see – did he come from Aspire, or something?'

'No,' said Pinch, sharply. 'And you needn't grin like that. It's not funny. Our father comes from the forest.'

Thomas stared at him. Why should that be a problem? The Gulls lived almost on the edge of the forest, and often went in there to gather herbs and mushrooms for Old Gal's mixtures.

'He is from the *deep* forest,' said Patch, with a strange smile. 'He's from the wild places. He doesn't like settled country. He's not even allowed to come into settled country, in fact.'

'He's got a gang,' cried Pinch. 'He's an outlaw!'

Patch said, sharply, 'Pinch, don't be silly.'

'Well, it's true,' said Pinch, defiantly.

Thomas said, slowly, 'Wow. I had no idea. How did your mother and he meet?'

'I think she was gathering herbs in the forest one day, further than she usually goes,' said Patch. 'Well, it wasn't meant to happen, but it did. They fell in love, and in secret, they got married. When the village found out, Mother was given a choice: give him up or give up her home. You see, when he was young, he and his men raided Owlchurch. They broke into Morph's Dream Emporium and let out a whole line of new dreams that Morph had only just bred up. He still holds a huge grudge, it took him ages to breed some more. Mother was lucky she *had* a choice. By rights she should have been exiled.'

'That's really mean,' said Thomas.

'That's how it's done here. But Angelica

Eyebright was Mother's friend. She thought Mother was very good at what she did. She didn't want to lose her.'

'That's good. But it must have been hard on your mother, to make that choice.'

Patch said, softly, 'Yes. And no. You see, she and Father – well they didn't get on, in the end. He was just too . . . too wild, and Mother's too proud. So they parted, and Mother stayed. She had us, and she worked hard. Things have never been easy for her. People in Owlchurch accept her now, but at first it was not easy.'

'And the people in Aspire despise her,' said Pinch, angrily. 'It's one of the reasons they think Owlchurch is inferior to them. They think she should have been drummed out, don't you see? *They* would not have hesitated!'

'I *do* see,' said Thomas, slowly. Things that had puzzled him in the past were becoming clearer. Not only what Hinkypunk had said, but also Old Gal's prickly pride, her standoffishness with the others in the village, as well as the Aspirants' attitude to the Gulls . . . He went on, gently, 'Your mother is very brave, I think.'

Pinch and Patch nodded. 'She is.'

'Do you . . . do you ever see your father?'

'Once a year,' said Patch, quietly.

'Mother takes us to a spot in the forest, and leaves us there,' said Pinch. He threw a stone into the water. 'We get to see him for only a short time. I wish we could see him more. But we're not allowed.'

'That's another thing,' said Patch. 'Angelica Eyebright allows us to do that, even though really we should never see him. But Mother herself isn't ever allowed to.'

'That's cruel,' cried Thomas.

'That's the way it is. And that's the way Mother wants it too,' said Patch, sternly.

'Well, I think it's awful,' said Thomas.

'Now you see why Mother can never get the Horns of Pan,' said Pinch. 'Not only do you have to be good at magic, but you have to have followed all the rules of the Hidden World. There's no two ways about it, as far as the Arkadians are concerned. You have to be perfect. And everyone suspects Owlchurch hasn't had another holder of the award in years because of Mother – because Angelica allowed her to stay. That's why Morph and all of them are so excited. If that means Mother has to suffer, too bad. Having a holder of the Horns of Pan is much more important.'

'Oh, it's all too silly! Who *wants* the dumb Horns of Pan?' cried Thomas, fiercely.

The twins looked at him, horrified. 'You mustn't say that!' said Pinch, in a low voice.

Thomas flushed. 'I'm just a human,' he said, defiantly. 'I don't have to follow your rules. Besides, *you* said, Pinch, that Pan was a bit of an old stick-in-the-mud.'

'Ssshh,' hissed Patch. 'You'll get us all into trouble, if anyone hears us!'

'It all just seems so unfair, so mean,' said

Thomas. 'And besides, I think there's something really fishy about it. I think we should do something.'

The twins stared. 'About what?'

'Everything,' said Thomas. 'Why should your mother have to suffer more? Why should you just meekly accept everything, just because it's the rules? Why should we let some pretty stranger walk in and take over? Let's do something about it!' He smiled at them. 'Just like we did in Pandemonium, Patch! You didn't just follow the rules, then, you thought for yourself!'

'Did I?' said Patch, wonderingly. 'I was scared, though.'

'So was I,' said Thomas.

'But you're a Rymer,' said Pinch, slowly. 'You can do all kinds of things we can't do.'

'What's stopping you?' said Thomas, fiercely. 'Come on, Pinch, you want to be clever, like Hinkypunk; do you think he always follows the rules?'

'No, but that's because he has Uncouther blood. He's not like the others.'

'And we don't *want* to be like Hinkypunk,' said Patch, firmly. 'He's clever, and he can be fun, but you can't always trust him.'

'You don't have to be *exactly* like him.' Thomas paused. 'Anyway, I don't think Hinkypunk is as keen on her as the others are.'

'So what? Hinkypunk's only ever keen on himself,' said Patch, crossly.

'Come on,' urged Thomas. 'You're not like the others, either. You have forest blood.'

'Green blood!' laughed Pinch.

'You can do different things to the others, because of that. Think about what that means.'

The twins looked thoughtful. 'Really?' said Pinch.

'Really,' said Thomas, firmly. And he was pleased to see his friends looked much more like their usual cheerful selves.

SEVEN

That evening, Thomas watched the Peree family carefully. They sat in the Apple Tree Café, the centre of an admiring group of villagers. Only the Gulls were not there. The Peree twins didn't say anything at all, just clung closely together, hand in hand, staring nervously at all the faces around them. Their mother was quite different, full of bright chatter. She didn't talk about her past or even of Arkadia, or how she had come to find herself in Owlchurch, but of what she was planning to do. And the more Thomas listened, the more he felt sure the Ariel meant to supplant Old Gal altogether. Or at the very least turn her into a servant. Once, she even let slip something that showed clearly she knew about Old Gal's past, but to Thomas's surprise, nobody asked her how she knew. The nagging feeling that he'd seen her somewhere was fading away. He must have made a mistake. There was simply no way he could have met the Ariel, and that was that. Probably he just thought he had because he didn't like her.

The others seemed quite, quite bewitched by her, especially Morph Onery. As to Thomas's dad, well, he couldn't stop looking at her. It made Thomas feel quite cross. Am I the only one here who doesn't trust her? he thought. What did that mean? Perhaps that he was being just mean and stubborn to perfectly innocent people . . . But really, it wasn't nice of the other Owlchurchers at all. Surely they didn't want to ditch Old Gal, just like that? For the first time he thought of Owlchurch with something like dislike. That was not a pleasant feeling at all.

* * *

He excused himself early and went up to bed in the small spare room. But he couldn't sleep, just kept tossing and turning, thinking of Pinch and Patch. He felt bad that he hadn't ever asked them about their father before. He'd never really thought about it. After all, his mother wasn't with *him*. But she was dead. That was very different . . .

He heard the Perees come up to bed, and his father settling them in. Then silence.

Thomas was nearly asleep himself when there was a sudden, small, sharp noise at the window. He sprang up and listened. There it came again! It was the rattling of pebbles against the glass. Thomas went to the window and looked out into the street. It was bright moonlight, and the Gull twins were standing there. Thomas signalled to them that he'd come down.

Hurriedly, he dressed and, holding his shoes in one hand, tiptoed in his socks to the stairs.

As he passed the Perees' room, he heard a soft voice, and froze, waiting for the fairy to come out of the room. But she didn't. She must be speaking to her children. He stayed in the corridor an instant, straining to hear what she said. But all he could catch was, 'Dawn . . . safe . . . don't worry . . .' Then there was silence.

He waited another instant, but nothing happened. He didn't want to be caught out here. And he had to see what the Gulls wanted. So he tiptoed downstairs and out into the street.

The twins looked cross. 'You took your time.'

Thomas slipped on his shoes. 'I had to make sure no one was going to come out. What's up?'

'We've decided you're right. We have to do *something*,' said Patch, dramatically. 'Before it's too late.'

'We decided we should go and talk to Father. He hears about very deep things, in the forest. He might know if something's up in Arkadia, and why that fairy's come here,' whispered Pinch, excitedly. 'And we want you to come with us!'

'*Will* you?' Patch said, anxiously.

Thomas grinned. 'Try and stop me!'

'Come on then, let's go,' said Pinch. 'If we hurry we can be back by dawn.'

'Dawn,' said Thomas. 'That reminds me. It probably doesn't mean much, but . . .' and he told them what he'd heard from behind the door.

'That makes it all the more important we should be back quickly,' said Patch. They hurried off, heading for the forest. Once or twice, Thomas looked behind them, to check that no one was following. Owlchurch stayed silent and peaceful, set in moonlight like a frozen scene on a screen.

But Thomas didn't have eyes in the back of his head. And so neither he nor the others saw the shadow that detached itself from the darkness behind Morph Onery's Dream

Emporium, and slunk towards the Apple Tree Café.

It was such a bright night that everything was almost as clear as day. They walked and walked. At first, the path was quite wide, and easy to walk along. But soon, it narrowed. The trees grew close together, their tops touching. There was less light here, and shadows striped the ground and lurked in the bushes. It was very quiet.

The dim quietness got to Thomas, after a while. He could feel the back of his neck prickling. He felt as if eyes were watching him from the shadows, but he could see nothing. The forest held its breath. Ahead of him, the twins scampered carelessly along. They didn't seem at all scared.

Suddenly, a bush to one side of the path moved. And another . . . Thomas gave a startled yelp, and swung around, only to see that another bush had sprung into his path.

There were eyes within the bushes, narrow, yellow, unblinking, *cold* eyes. He could feel the coldness seep into his very bones.

Then he heard Pinch's voice, high, nervous but trying to be steady, 'Come on, it's only us, we've come to see the Man.'

A bush spoke – or rather, growled, 'You have a stranger with you.'

'He's a friend. A Rymer.'

The leading bush shook itself, and turned into a short, squat creature with skin the texture and colour of bark, a shock of hair in which twigs and leaves mixed, and rough-spun breeches and tunic in woodsy colours. The cold eyes fixed on Thomas. The creature growled, 'A Rymer? We haven't seen one of those for a while. The wood is full of *strange wonders* these days.' It grinned in a rather sinister manner.

Pinch didn't seem worried. 'Will you take us to our father, please, Mr Bosky? Mr Bosky works for our father,' he explained to Thomas, lightly.

'Hmm. Very well,' said Bosky, still suspiciously. He had teeth as yellow as his eyes, but pointed and sharp. They made Thomas feel queasy.

The three outlaws surrounded Thomas and the twins like a guard. They marched them down the path, and then off it, into a thicket so tangled that Thomas had his hands and face thoroughly scratched before they managed to get through it. At the other side of the thicket was a grassy clearing. At one end of the clearing was a mound against which grew a thick, twisted tree, covered in leaves. Nothing unusual about that, except for the fact the leaves were of many colours, from the sheerest green to the darkest brown, and every leafy shade in between: gold, pale yellow, red, scarlet, deep green. There were even some leaves that were only lacy skeletons. It was as if every season was happening at the same time on that tree.

Bosky tapped three times on the tree's rough

bark. There was a grinding, tearing sound, and part of the trunk slid to one side, revealing a dark passageway beyond.

The children went in behind the silent outlaws. The trunk closed behind them, and all at once they were in darkness. Thomas's heart hammered. There was a strange smell in there; a smell part musty, part animal. Then a light was struck; and Bosky's harsh voice said, 'Follow me.'

Through the dark passageway they walked, and then into a dimly-lit hall. Bosky said, 'Wait here,' and he went off through a door at the far end, followed by his friends. Thomas and the twins were left alone.

'Oh! It's so beautiful . . .' murmured Thomas. The room was an airy space hung with rich green and gold tapestries, and with green and gold carpets on the floor. In one corner, a heap of green and gold cushions were piled. Tapestries, cushions and carpets shimmered and rustled like living things —

or like, he realised suddenly, the leafy heads of trees.

'Pinch,' he said, 'you didn't tell me—' But he never finished his sentence, for just then the door opened and an extraordinary figure strode into the room, surrounded by the outlaws.

EIGHT

He was huge. His head almost touched the ceiling, but his frame was twisted and misshapen. And he was almost completely green. His clothes were made of patchworks of leaves. Instead of hair, wild tangles of branches and vines and leaves grew out from the sides of his head, and down his chin. But his features were regular, even noble, with a finely-shaped mouth and nose, and rather sad light brown eyes.

'Children,' he said, in a soft, deep voice, 'why are you here? Your mother did not send word of your coming.'

Pinch quavered, 'She doesn't know we're here, Father. We . . . we needed to see you.'

'There are bad things happening, Father,' put in Patch, shyly.

'We need your advice,' went on Pinch.

'Your help,' capped Patch. She added, 'Father, this is our friend, Thomas Trew. True Tom. He's a Rymer, Father!'

The giant bent down to Thomas. 'Pleased to meet you, Rymer. I am these urchins' father. My name is Vertome, the Green Man. Welcome to my part of the forest.

'It is a pleasure to see a Rymer in my woods again. It has been a long time. A merry day to you, Rymer.'

'And to you, sir,' stammered Thomas, quite overwhelmed.

'Ah, Rymer! If it could be a merry day for the likes of me again! But the springtime of the world has gone, mischief no longer forgiven. And so I am an outlaw. No matter, no matter. That is the way of the world.' He turned to his men. 'Acorn! Bosky! Skrob!' he snapped. 'Bring food, bring drink.' He gestured at the cushions.

'Come, children, let us sit down. Tell me what has happened.'

He bent his great frame down, slowly, like a toppling tree, into the cushions. He leant back into them, and groaned. 'There, that's better. Ah, my back aches, these days!' The children perched around him. He said, 'You have grown, Pinch and Patch.'

'Yes, Father.'

'So tell me. What was so urgent you needed to break the rules to see me?' His voice was stern, but there was a dancing sparkle in his eyes.

Patch whispered, 'Father, strange things are going on in Owlchurch.'

The Green Man threw back his head and laughed. 'Strange things, child? Isn't that always the way, in places where people live packed together like ants in a mound?' He spoke as if Owlchurch was a city, thought Thomas. What would he say if he saw London?

'Well, Father, there's this Ariel woman . . .' Quickly, Patch sketched in what had happened, with many interruptions from Pinch. The Green Man listened. 'I see,' he said. 'Well, I'm afraid it does sound as though the Peree woman is to take your mother's place. After all, Old Gal does not have the Horns of Pan, and never can. It does rather trump everything else, doesn't it? No, if Pan has spoken by granting her this, you should leave well alone, my children. It's the law, after all. Or else who knows what you may stir up?'

The twins looked crestfallen. 'But, Father . . .' began Pinch.

'You thought that because I was an outlaw, I would tell you to ignore this law?' said the Green Man, in a quiet, rather dangerous voice. 'How little you must know me. Arkadia is respected by us all.'

The twins flushed and looked miserable. Hotly, Thomas said, 'No, sir. They did *not* think that. They thought you might be able to help, that you might know something about . . . Oh! You must see it is all quite unjust! Old Gal – the twins' mother . . . your wife . . . er, I mean, she has worked very hard, all her life. Owlchurch has been happy to use her skills.'

The Green Man looked thoughtfully at him. 'You could all leave Owlchurch. I always said villages were bad places.'

'I'd love to . . .' began Pinch, but Patch quelled him with a glare.

Thomas said, 'They can't do that, sir. Owlchurch is their home. And it's become mine, too. We're not against Frodite Peree coming to stay. We just don't see why she should be allowed to take everything from Old Gal. It's just not fair. Besides, we're not even sure she's genuine!'

'Hmm,' said the Green Man. 'Fairness has nothing to do with it, in the Hidden World, my boy. As to the other . . .' His brows knitted. 'She has the Horns of Pan. It's true that there have been few granted, recently. But that honour has never been lightly given.'

'Then . . .'

'If you are speaking against a genuine holder of the Horns of Pan, I'd advise you to stop right away, or face exile for ever from the Hidden World.'

'But can't a genuine holder of the Horns of Pan be a bad person?'

'They can. But that does not matter. If it is genuine . . . then, *whatever* Frodite Peree does – except if she allows Uncouthers up into the village – must be endured, for she cannot be stopped. You either endure it, or leave Owlchurch. But there is a possibility . . .' He paused.

'What?' said Pinch, in an agony of impatience.

'There is just a faint, a remote possibility, that somehow, she has obtained the genuine thing, by trickery. It has been heard of but long ago,' said the Green Man, carefully, 'and the culprits were caught and severely punished. Few in the Hidden World would risk such a thing. The Arkadians are respected by all, and they have always strictly punished breaches of their law.'

'Not even the Uncouthers would do this?' said Thomas.

'I think not even them.'

'But what if it's a human who's done it?' said Thomas. 'A human wouldn't feel the same way about it, would they?'

Everyone looked at him. 'No. But I don't really think it's possible for a human to do it, anyway,' said the Green Man, slowly.

'But you're not *sure*, sir?' said Thomas, hopefully.

Vertome laughed for the first time. 'You are a persistent young fellow,' he said. 'It's *just* possible, I suppose. But only if that person were to be a highly gifted magician, *and* had help from someone powerful – and ruthless – in the Hidden World.'

'Oh!' said Patch, eagerly. 'We've got to get

back and tell everyone, before it's too late.'

'Child, child,' said the Green Man, shaking his head, 'it isn't as simple as that. You must know for sure; you cannot accuse without proof. In fact, I would advise you to drop the whole thing, and make your peace with the Perees. Living as an outlaw is one thing for an old man like me – but you are young, and you would find it dreadful indeed.' He saw their stubborn faces, and sighed. 'Very well. If you won't do that, then there is only one thing to do. You must gather your proof. You must go to Arkadia and ask Pan himself if he *has* granted this honour to the Peree creature.'

They all stared at him. Thomas said, 'But I thought Arkadia was far away. And we really need to get back to Owlchurch quickly!'

'There *is* a very quick way to get there,' said the Green Man. 'On a unicorn's back.'

'On a unicorn!' exclaimed Pinch. 'But, Father . . .'

'Yes, I know, they're cross and flighty beasts,'

said his father. 'But there's nothing beats 'em for speed. You'd be there and back in no time. And I know just the one – Silverhair. A silly, giddy creature, but she owes me a favour. She'll take you as far as the Syrinx River, the border of Arkadia, anyway, and bring you back, too.'

'A unicorn!' said Patch, suddenly remembering what she'd seen that morning. But before she could speak, Pinch interrupted. His face was bright with glee. 'Can we leave right away, Father? Can we?'

'Very well,' said the Green Man, looking at their eager faces. 'You can. Bosky will take you out again, and call Silverhair. Take care, my children – Arkadia is beautiful but can be dangerous, if you don't know what you're doing. Do not attempt to question Pan's judgement. If he has given this honour to the Peree woman, he will not like it if you criticise her. Speak carefully, and very politely. And be ready for the unexpected.'

NINE

Back in the grassy clearing outside, Bosky made the children climb a big oak. 'Best be safe than sorry,' he growled. As soon as they were up in the spreading branches, he took a little flute out of his pocket and, putting it to his lips, appeared to blow hard into it. But they could hear no sound.

Pinch nudged Thomas. 'Unicorns hear at a very high pitch.'

'Like dogs in my world,' said Thomas, nodding.

Bosky was listening, head to one side. Then he put the flute to his lips again.

'I think I can hear it coming,' said Patch,

wriggling a little on her branch. She looked half-scared, half-excited. 'There's something I have to tell you . . .'

But she never finished her sentence, for suddenly, the air filled with a loud drumming sound, followed by a thin, high, shrill, unearthly scream. In the next moment, Bosky himself was up the tree. He grinned at them. 'She's coming and she's in a towering temper,' he said. 'Watch out, my dears.'

The drumming sound was getting louder. The shrill scream came again. Thomas's heart beat faster and faster.

And suddenly, there she was, skidding into the clearing, right under the oak tree, blowing loudly through her flared nostrils, her silver-white coat so bright it seemed to be sending out sparks. Her glittering green eyes rolled in her head, her mane stood out on end. She gave her scream again – much louder than before. The awful sound seemed to drill into Thomas's skull. He hardly heard Patch's whisper, 'It *is* the same one!'

Bosky peered down through the leaves and said, lightly, 'My, my, but the day has not agreed with you, Silverhair!'

The unicorn swivelled her head from side to side, clearly looking for the owner of the voice. 'They're so short-sighted they're almost blind,' whispered Pinch in Thomas's ear.

The unicorn blew hard, and hot steam came out of her nostrils. She spoke. 'Woodman, show yourself.' Her voice was a surprise. It should have sounded like a horse's, like her scream did – high, whinnying, nerve-wracking. But it was soft, deep, almost growly. It made strange prickles come out all over Thomas's skin. He wasn't sure if they were prickles of fear, or delight.

'Our mutual friend bids you good day, and asks for your help, Silverhair.'

The unicorn stood still. Her eyes sharpened. 'It is true I owe the Man,' she said, at last.

'You do.' Bosky slid down the tree, and

dropped down at the unicorn's feet. The silver hoofs flashed – but only as the animal took a wary step back.

'Silverhair, you're to take some passengers to Arkadia.' Bosky leant against the tree, smiling.

The unicorn stiffened. She lifted her head and looked up into the tree. Somehow, her expression made Thomas shiver. 'Passengers?' she said. 'Arkadia?'

'You heard,' said Bosky, casually. 'Come on, children. Down you come. She won't bite – now.'

The unicorn struck with a hoof at the ground, sending out cold fire. 'Take care, woodman. I am no ordinary unicorn, but of the ancient and worshipful clan of Reem-Hornaz.'

Bosky shrugged. 'We know. That is why the Man thought of asking you, above all other unicorns. Not everyone is as welcome to cross the Syrinx as you are, Silverhair.'

The unicorn's manner changed at once. She

became almost coy. 'Very well. Where are my passengers?'

Bosky beckoned them down. 'Here,' said Pinch, sliding down the tree. 'And here,' said Patch, sliding down in her turn. 'Then there's me,' said Thomas, clambering carefully down.

'The Man's children,' said Bosky, comfortably, 'and a human, a Rymer.'

The unicorn stared at Thomas. 'My stars,' she said, slowly. 'To think that it's true!'

'Is what true?' said Bosky, sharply.

'Why, that they exist. To think that . . .'

'Don't think,' said Bosky. 'It'll make your head ache. Just take them to Arkadia, Silverhair, please.'

The unicorn was still staring at the children. Those eyes really give me the creeps, thought Thomas. He stole a glance at the Gull twins. Patch looked a bit sick, but Pinch stared back defiantly.

'Very well,' said the unicorn, at last. 'I'll do this for the Man. Jump on my back, then. And hold on to my mane. We'll take off right away.'

It was surprisingly comfortable too, on the unicorn's back. In fact, it was almost as comfortable as sitting on a broad, deep chair.

Silverhair growled, 'Ready? Hang on tight, and close your eyes – or you will be sick.'

They obeyed, feeling nervous and excited. Pinch murmured, 'They go so fast it's almost a kind of flying, you see,' and Patch whispered back, 'Just imagine if they could see us back in Owlchurch.'

'We'd be in mighty big trouble if they could,' said Pinch.

Thomas was about to say something, when all at once, he felt a great lurch, and a huge sucking feeling, like a plane taking off very fast. His ears filled with shrill screaming, his head lightened, and darkness rushed up under his eyelids. He only just had time to think, oh no, what's happening to me? when he fainted and knew no more.

TEN

He came to with wind rushing into his mouth and an ache pounding in his head. Cautiously, he tried to open his eyes, but they were gummed shut. His cheeks felt cold.

'Thomas?' It was Patch's anxious voice. 'Are you all right?'

'I think so,' he whispered back. 'What happened?'

'She took off a bit too fast. She's a bit of a reckless flyer, this one.' That was Pinch. 'We think that— Ow!' he yelped, as the unicorn came to a sudden, jarring stop.

Thomas's ears popped. His face felt stretched like a piece of elastic. His teeth and head ached. His limbs felt weak. He let go of the mane and fell headlong off the unicorn's back, landing on something soft. He tried to open his eyes but they were still gummed shut. He heard Pinch's yell. 'She's thrown us off! Hey, no! Hey, you, come back!' But there was no answer, only the drumming of the unicorn's hoofs, disappearing into the distance.

'Pinch . . . Patch . . .' whispered Thomas. 'Where are you? I can't see anything. I think I've gone blind!'

'Here . . .' Thomas felt their light, dry little hands on his own. 'It's OK,' said Patch's voice. He felt a light touch on his eyes. 'Don't panic. You're not really blind. Wait. I've got a little jar of one of Mother's patent ointments. Let me rub it on.'

He could feel it gliding on to his eyes like a trickle of cool water. Suddenly, his eyes flew open. He could see . . .

And there were the Gull twins, smiling

anxiously at him, even Pinch, who was rarely anxious. 'How do you feel?'

Thomas felt himself, gingerly. 'OK, I think. My head aches a bit, though.'

'Something spooked her,' said Patch. 'Like it did this morning.'

'This morning?'

Patch explained what she'd seen. 'I think there's something wrong with her,' she finished.

'There sure is. She's crazy,' snapped Pinch. 'We should have known better than to rely on a *unicorn*.'

'I think she's *gone* crazy,' agreed Patch. 'Something happened to her, in the forest. She's not behaving normally at all.'

'Where are we?' said Thomas, looking around. They'd landed in a forest glade of some sort; the grass was soft underfoot, the trees towered above them. He could hear the silver sound of a stream somewhere close by. It should have been a beautiful place. But it felt odd, somehow. Wrong . . .

'I'm not sure,' said Patch. 'But I think that water we can hear – I think it's the Syrinx. So she's brought us where she said she would.'

'But why didn't she—' Thomas broke off, staring. 'Look!' he pointed.

There, at the far end of the glade, something shimmered. Something caught in a silver net of light. It was . . . it was a *bow*, held taut in a shining white hand, and there was an *arrow*, fitted to the bow!

'Run!' he shouted. 'Run like crazy!' And he took to his heels, heading straight for the undergrowth, Pinch and Patch scampering bewildered after him.

Not a moment too soon; for just as they plunged deep into the dark thickets, an arrow flashed through the air, and thudded into a tree-trunk not far away. Then came another – and another!

'We've got to do something,' whispered Thomas, quickly. 'We can't just stay here waiting to be turned into pincushions.' He was thinking of a story he'd once read, about an angry immortal huntress who shot any trespassers rash enough to intrude into her private glade. 'We should do a thinning spell.'

Patch and Pinch stared at him. He went on, quickly, 'Come on, let's hold hands, let's do the spell, now, I'll explain later!'

Thinning is an odd sensation. At first, your mouth goes numb – a bit like getting an injection at the dentist's. The numbness spreads. You touch your hand, and it feels like it doesn't belong to you. You put your hand to your side, and it feels like it's not there. Then, all at once, there's a prickling feeling, pins and needles breaking out everywhere. You can *feel* your body now, but you can't see it at all. Then the pins and needles stop, but if you're human, you begin to feel itchy. The itch gets worse and worse the longer you stay invisible. It starts to drive you mad.

Hidden Worlders don't get the itch, and they can stay invisible for quite a long time.

But even they get bad effects, eventually – dizziness and giddiness. That's because 'thinning' is not only a spell, it's a kind of place. You're sandwiched in between the worlds, in a kind of limbo space. It's foggy and white in there, and you can't see a thing, at first. Sometimes there are ghosts in there. They brush past your face like sticky cobwebs. And it's cold. Very cold. All in all, not a pleasant place to be.

But it would do to hide in for a little while, and at least they could see out into the world outside without being seen. So the twins and Thomas held tight to each other's hands, and waited, holding their breath. No more arrows came flying.

'I wonder who that person was . . .' said Patch, at last.

'I think I can guess,' said Thomas.

'Who?'

'I read a story once, about a great Lady of the forest, a huntress who doesn't like trespassers.'

'Oh, great,' wailed Pinch. After a pause, he went on, 'Silverhair dumped us here on purpose, so this Arkadian Lady could turn us into pincushions! Wait till Father hears of her treachery!'

'No. I think Patch is right,' said Thomas. 'That unicorn is all nerves. She isn't thinking straight.'

'When does a unicorn ever do that?' grumbled Pinch.

'There was a strange look in her eyes – like she wasn't focused properly, like she was almost *bewitched*.'

'But who would do that?' squeaked Patch, then she put a hand over her mouth. 'Everyone knows the rules about unicorns. You're not *allowed* to enchant them. You don't think . . . you don't think it's the Perees?'

'We can't blame *everything* on them,' said Thomas, fairly. 'Besides, what reason would there be for it?'

'To get us shot by that archer,' snapped Pinch.

'How would they know we're here? They're back in the village. They don't even know we're gone. Anyway, question is, what are we going to do, right now? If Pinch is right and the stream we heard is the Syrinx, then we have to pass through the glade to get to Arkadia. But how, without being shot full of arrows? We can't stay thinned for long. But if we pop back, she'll see us!' He paused. 'What do you two know about how things work in Arkadia?'

'Not a lot really,' said Patch, after a little silence. 'The Arkadians are respected by all the rest of the Hidden World, but they don't take much notice of what happens elsewhere. They think Arkadia is the best place in the Hidden World.'

'And they've got some of the oldest magic,' said Pinch, adding gloomily, 'None of that is very useful, is it?'

'Wait,' said Patch. 'I remember something else. Arkadians love pretty things. Maybe we should give this person something pretty?'

'That's all very well,' snorted Pinch, 'but what are you suggesting? And no, *you* won't do, Patch!'

'Oh, ha, ha,' said Patch, crossly. 'Very funny, I *don't* think!'

'Hang on,' said Thomas. 'I know. Let's empty our pockets. Pinch – what do you have?'

'I've got some skimming stones, a leaf, oh – half of an old biscuit, a frog skin . . . and that's all.'

'And I've got Mother's jar, and a feather, and two pebbles – they're really pretty,' said Patch, hopefully.

'And I've got a pencil . . . and wait – the pack of cards! I forgot to take them out of my trousers pocket after we'd been playing, yesterday.'

'Oh, yes!' said the twins, together. Pinch added, 'That's it! All the other things – you can probably find them in Arkadia. But a pack of cards, from the Obbo world – bet they don't have one. And they're pretty. Plus you could teach them a card game . . .'

'We have to do something, and fast,' said Patch. 'We can't stay thinned too much longer.'

'No,' said Thomas. He had a terrible burning itch under one arm, now, like a fire under his skin. 'We've got to try it.' He gripped their hands. 'Well?'

'We're ready,' said the Gull twins, in solemn, scared voices.

'OK, we're going to creep, really quietly, back to the glade. Once we're there, I'm going to take out the cards. I'm going to sit at the edge of the glade, and spread out the cards on the grass. I'm going to start playing Patience.'

'But what if she tries to shoot you?'

'I won't think about that. I think she'll be curious to see what I'm doing. After all, I won't be trying to get into the glade, just sitting there, quietly playing cards. I reckon she must get bored or lonely. Maybe she'll get interested in the cards.'

'Oh, Thomas!' said Patch. 'You're so brave, and clever.'

Thomas blushed. No one could see it, but he could feel it flaming in his cheeks. He stammered, 'I'm not. It's just – we have to do something. And we can't give up, not now.'

'Hope you're right, then,' said Pinch, in a small voice. 'Rather you than me.'

ELEVEN

It seemed to take for ever, slowly and quietly creeping back. But after a while, they were at the edge of the glade. They were still thinned, but it would not be long before they had to break out of it.

No more arrows shot out, but the glade was full of that strange light. Thomas could feel a presence there, though he couldn't see her. He squeezed the twins' hands, and whispered, 'You should come out of thinning now, but stay hidden. I'll just stay thinned a moment longer, all right?'

He heard their voices, little more than breaths in his ear. 'Yes.'

He dropped their hands and walked slowly

forward. Any minute, he expected an arrow to skewer him. He was 'thinned' but was that really a protection against the old, old Arkadian magic, or had the Huntress just not bothered to hunt them down? He could feel his heart pounding in his chest, and the presence in the glade growing stronger and stronger. It was the hardest, most frightening thing he'd done in his life, scarier even than his experiences in the Uncouthers' kingdom.

He sat down on the soft grass. No sound, though he could feel eyes watching him. He brought out his pack of cards. They weren't 'thinned' of course, but quite visible. Hands shaking, he dealt them out into five piles, face-down. He turned up the first card on the first pack. It was a Queen of hearts. He turned up the first card on the second pile. It was a King of hearts. There was still complete silence in the glade. He turned up the first card on the third pile. It was the Jack of hearts! Now he almost forgot the Huntress, so amazed was he at turning up all the highest-value cards. He turned up the first card in the fourth pile. It was an Ace of hearts. 'Well,' he said, aloud, without thinking, 'if I turn up the ten on this last pile, it must mean I'm really very lucky indeed today. Or this glade is full of the most wonderful magic.' Too late, he'd realised what he'd done, and looked around fearfully. But no one said anything, no bowstring twanged, nothing at all happened. Yet he had the feeling someone was watching, waiting, breathlessly, wanting to know what would happen next. It made him feel better.

He turned over the first card on the last pile. The ten of hearts! What an amazing thing! He shuffled off those first cards, and put them away. Then he turned up the second card in the first pile. An Ace of spades! He turned up the next card in the second pile: the King of spades! 'This is unreal,' he muttered, and was about to turn over the next card in the third pile when a voice spoke, quite close to him.

'I'd say you had either Fate working with you – or you're cheating. Which is it?'

Thomas jumped. The voice was not what he had expected. It was very young, for a start.

'Er . . . er . . .' he began, but she went on,' It's all right. I'm not going to hurt you. I didn't mean to, anyway.'

You could have fooled us, Thomas thought, but didn't say. 'Lady of the Hunt,' he said aloud, in a low, respectful voice, 'we are friends of your great people, come from Middler lands on the other side of the forest to—'

'Stop right there,' said the voice, and suddenly someone popped into view, right next to Thomas. It was not the tall, elegant Huntress he'd imagined, but a little girl, shorter than Thomas and not a great deal taller than Patch. She had a head of wild red-brown hair and a very pale face. Her eyes were a strange colour, almost purple. She wore a thin grey tunic and her rather dirty feet were bare. In one hand she carried a bow. In his surprise,

Thomas forgot his manners.

'Who *are* you?'

The girl frowned. 'I should ask the questions. It's *my* home you've trespassed in. Besides, I won't answer someone I can't even see.'

'Sorry,' said Thomas, and with great relief, he

burst out of 'thinning'. It was like a punch in the chest that threw him off his feet, tumbling on to the grass. His skin felt tight and hot. He scrambled to his feet. The girl looked at him.

'So there *you* are. You're just a boy!'

'So?' said Thomas.

'I thought you were some great magician, trying to get uninvited into Arkadia. You went invisible, you bewitched Silverhair and—'

'We did *not* bewitch that silly unicorn,' said Thomas, crossly. 'She was meant to take us right across the Syrinx, but she threw us off before she reached it. I think there's something wrong with her.'

The girl stared at him. 'Meant to take *us*? Who's *us*?'

'Me – I'm called Thomas, Thomas Trew – and my friends Pinch and Patch Gull. Their father is the Green Man and he was the one who told Silverhair to bring us here.'

'Why didn't you say so from the start,' broke

in the girl, crossly. 'The Green Man is always welcome in Arkadia.' She looked around. 'But where are your friends?'

'Here,' said the Gull twins with one voice, stepping forward out of hiding.

The girl stared at them. 'I suppose I can see a look of your father,' she allowed, grandly.

'That's big of you,' said Pinch, rather crankily. Thinning didn't really agree with his temper. 'You could have asked us who we were before trying to kill us.'

'And you could have said who you were before you came flying into my glade without asking,' said the girl, sharply. 'That was bound to make me suspicious. There have been some strange characters trying to wriggle their way into our country in the past, you know.'

'We are humbly sorry,' said Thomas, hastily, 'really we are, Lady of the Hunt.'

'Stop calling me that,' snapped the girl, 'that's the title they gave to my grandmother Diana, who no longer lives in Arkadia but retired to

Ariel lands a long time ago. I'm Selena. You don't know much, do you?'

'No,' said Thomas, trying to sound humble. He caught the twins' eye, willing Pinch, especially, to stay quiet. He did, but his scornful expression said it all. The Arkadians were as bad as the Aspirants, he was thinking.

'Why do you want to go to Arkadia?' said Selena.

'We need to humbly ask the great Pan a question,' said Thomas. 'It is a matter of great importance to us, and to Arkadia as well, I'd say.' He paused, then plunged on, 'Lady Selena, we were wondering if you might perhaps, in your infinite kindness and wisdom, take us across the Syrinx River and take us to see King Pan.'

The girl's eyes narrowed. 'Maybe,' she allowed. 'But first . . .' and she pointed at the forgotten cards on the ground '. . . first you have to teach me how to do this.'

'You know about these games?' said Thomas,

carefully. Selena tossed her head. 'Of course. There have been visitors in Arkadia from other lands, you know. One even taught me a game of cards, like yours. But I have never seen anyone doing what you did. Teach me how it's done!'

Fat chance, thought Thomas. It was just a fluke. But he sat down with her and the Gull twins – who looked just as eager as she did – reshuffled the cards, and carefully divided them into five piles, once again. Nothing would work out this time, he was sure of it.

TWELVE

Perhaps it was indeed that the glade had its own magic, or perhaps because he was just very lucky that day, but he managed once again to turn up all the suits of cards, one after the other. Selena was thrilled, and the Gulls impressed. Then Selena had to have a go, and Thomas held his breath. Would she be angry if she couldn't do it just like Thomas, and threaten to shoot them again?

Luckily, he didn't have to find out. She turned up the right cards, one after the other. But when the Gulls tried, the cards wouldn't perform. They looked very cross at this, and muttered darkly about unfair Arkadian magic. Selena took no notice. She swept all the cards up into her hand and said, wistfully, 'I've never played so well before. Oh how I'd like cards just like these!'

'Have them,' said Thomas, hastily. 'They're a gift, from us to you, Selena, for taking us to the great Pan himself.'

'Really?' Selena's purple eyes glowed with light. She clutched the pack to her heart. 'Oh, thank you!'

Pinch grumbled something, but not out loud. Patch looked at the ground and shuffled her feet. Thomas knew they were regretting giving the cards, already, though they'd agreed it was the thing to do. He wanted to tell them not to worry, that he could easily get more, but he knew they wouldn't believe him. And in truth he was rather sad at giving that pack up, especially after it had worked for him so well just now. Still, that probably had something to do with the place here more than anything. Maybe the grass itself, where they'd lain?

* * *

Moving on, they came to the stream. At first sight, it was more of a brook than a river – a sparkling little stream of water that ran over mossy stones. But Selena said, 'Hold on to my waist, Thomas, and you two, hold on to him. It's deeper than it looks.'

That was true. As soon as they stepped into the water, it began to move up their legs. Before they were in the middle of it, it was up to their waists, and moving much faster than they could have imagined, the current sucking at their bodies. By the time they were safely on the opposite side, they were feeling quite frightened, their legs rather weak. Selena smiled when she saw their expression.

'That's one of the ways we keep unwelcome strangers out,' she said, brightly.

'And shooting them full of arrows too, I suppose,' grumbled Pinch. Selena just laughed.

Beyond the stream, the path was narrow at first, but soon widened into a wide, sunlit track. The forest lapped on either side of it, but it was a different-looking forest now. It was more like beautiful parkland. Big trees, some heavily-laden with golden fruit, grew here and there, with smaller flowering shrubs in between. The grass was green and long and very soft, and the air smelt of perfume. Soon, they began to see a few houses scattered here and there amongst the big trees – including some actually *up* trees. Then they began to catch glimpses of people.

'That's a dryad, they're tree-dwellers,' whispered Pinch to him, as they passed a strange, thin person with stick-like arms, long green hair, and a long sad face. In fact, she looked a bit like Old Gal. 'And there's a nymph, see, sitting by that stream, combing her hair. Pretty, isn't she?'

'Oh, and look, how cute!' said Patch, low. 'A faun!' The little creature, like a cross between a child and a baby goat, was indeed rather cute. But it stuck out a long thin tongue rather rudely at them as they went past.

'Where there's fauns, there's satyrs, too – watch out, they are often rather rough and tipsy and they like to play stupid jokes,' threw Selena, over her shoulder. But despite her warning, they didn't meet any of the big horned and hairy men; instead, round a corner in the track, they came face to face with something much rarer and awesome: a centaur. The majestic creature was dozing at the door of his home, a rough, large shelter of big logs. He had masses of black, tangled hair, a large moustache and beard, and massive shoulders and torso. His waist ended in a powerful draughthorse's body as black as his hair. As they went past, he opened one eye. It was of a mild, bright blue.

'Greetings, Chironel,' said Selena. Thomas noticed she bowed most politely, so he bowed too, as did the Gulls.

The centaur opened the other eye. 'Greetings, child,' he said in a rather

whinnying voice. His glance swept over the
others. 'And who are our visitors?'

'From a Middler country,' said Selena. 'They
want to speak to Pan.'

'A Middler country, eh? They're coming

thick and fast, these days, after ignoring us for so long,' said the centaur, slowly rolling to his feet. At full size, he towered over the children.

'Have you had other visitors, then, sir, from our part of the world?' dared Thomas.

'Why, yes, I believe that's where they were from – the woman and her husband who passed by here not several days ago.'

Thomas and the twins looked at each other. 'Sir,' went on Thomas, 'was she beautiful, with long golden hair and blue eyes? Was she wearing a green dress the colour of beech leaves and a cloak of silver?'

'Why yes, the very one,' said the centaur, cheerfully. 'Do you know her?'

'Yes,' said Thomas, rather crestfallen. So Frodite Peree *had* been to Arkadia after all!

But Patch had listened carefully to what the centaur had said earlier. She said, 'Sir, you said she had a husband.'

'So I did. So she did,' said the centaur, mildly.

'At least I think he was. I do not think he was a servant – he seemed to be most familiar with her.'

'She had no children?'

'No,' said the centaur. 'Of course, she may have children,' he added. 'But she didn't bring them here.'

'What did her husband look like?' said Pinch, eagerly.

'Didn't see much of him,' said Chironel, casually. 'He wore a heavy coat with a hood. Think he was masked, too. Can't say I was interested. All sorts of strange types have been here.'

The twins and Thomas looked at each other. Not only did Frodite Peree not have a husband in tow now, but she had not said a word about him in Owlchurch. What had happened to him?

'Sir,' said Thomas, carefully, 'do you know what they were doing, here in Arkadia?'

'No idea,' said the centaur, yawning. 'Now, if

you don't mind, my Middler friends, I find I'm still very tired, and—'

'Sir, did she wear the Horns of Pan?' Thomas cut in, quickly.

The centaur stared at him. 'Horns of Pan?'

'Sir, as a crest.'

'She had no crest,' said the centaur, heavily, sinking slowly to his feet. 'She carried no shield and there was nothing on her cloak.'

'A bracelet? A necklace?' persisted Thomas.

'I saw nothing,' grunted the centaur, folding his arms and putting his head down on them.

'You are sure – she had no Horns of Pan?'

'Told you so, didn't I? You're as bad as a horsefly, child,' said the centaur, closing his eyes.

'But do you think – do you think she might have gone to petition Pan for it to be granted to her?'

'Our King doesn't hand out honours like fallen acorns, boy,' said Chironel, very crossly now. 'They aren't given to any old blow-ins, you know. They have to be earned, and there's a whole ceremony attached to the bestowing of the honour. I always attend such ceremonies, and I can tell you there's been none such in Arkadia in quite a long time.'

Triumphantly the twins and Thomas looked at each other, 'Thank you, sir. Oh thank you,' Thomas said. 'We won't bother you any more.'

'Better not,' said the centaur, and he turned his head away from them and gave a light snore.

All this time, Selena had been standing silent, looking a little indignant and a little scared. Now she whispered, 'I've never heard the lord Chironel speak so much, you are lucky indeed.' She looked as though, between the 'magic' cards and the centaur's words, she had rapidly changed her mind about just how important these visitors might be.

'You understand why we need to see the lord Pan, then,' said Pinch, very grandly indeed. 'This fraud has been using the good name of

Pan in vain, and sowing havoc and discord in our country.'

'Wait a minute,' said Thomas. 'We can't be sure she is a fraud. Remember what your father said.'

Pinch and Patch looked at him in astonishment. 'Don't be silly,' snapped Pinch. 'Of course she is. Selena, lead us on to Pan!'

'If you like,' said the girl, a little uncertainly. 'But I warn you – take good care in what you say. There has not been a theft of the Horns of Pan for a long time, and Pan's anger may be very great, as his pride will be wounded.'

'Lead on,' repeated Pinch. 'We can deal with all that, can't we, Thomas? Thomas is a Rymer, remember, and we're the children of the Green Man.'

'And of Old Gal Gull,' said Patch, flicking her brother a sharp glance. 'Never forget Mother, Pinch.'

'Who says I am?' groused Pinch.

'Just don't forget,' repeated Patch, stubbornly.

THIRTEEN

Nobody seemed to work, in Arkadia. People lounged around on soft grass, or blew on little flutes, or flitted through the trees in the moonlight that was almost as bright as day. There were no fields, no orchards, no barns; no shops, no churches or cafés or workshops. Yet everyone looked well-fed, healthy, and happy. The whole air was saturated with magic. Everything must just come to them without effort of any kind. And no one seemed to have any curiosity about the visitors whatever. Perhaps that was why Thomas and the twins began to feel the place was beautiful, but rather dull. What was there really to *do* here?

The path wound down, and they descended some rock steps to a little waterfall. Beside it was a large white cave. And at the entrance to the cave sat a person Thomas recognised at once, though he'd never seen him before. 'It's Pan!'

He was a short, stocky creature, dressed in a green sleeveless tunic, and a fur cape over that. He had a man's head and upper body, with strong, muscly arms protruding from the tunic. Beneath it were the hairy legs and hoofs of a goat. A pair of curling horns, decorated with scented white flowers, protruded from his forehead. He had very black hair and a little pointy beard. Bright yellow-brown eyes sparkled in his mischievous, handsome face. Surrounded by pretty, chattering nymphs, he lay sprawled on a fur rug.

The nymphs all stopped chattering when they saw Thomas and the twins, and stared at them. But Pan said, casually, 'Why, Selena, you bring us visitors! How charming.'

'They're Middlers, Sire,' she said, curtseying. 'Oh, and he's a Rymer. They've come from Owlchurch, on the far side of the forest, to ask you a question, Sire. Seems there's a holder of the Horns of Pan newly arrived in their village.'

'Really?' said Pan, eyebrows raised. 'Are you not happy with such a signal honour to your little tin-pot village, wherever it is?'

Thomas disliked his tone. Besides, the place got on his nerves, he was hungry and thirsty, and he couldn't wait to get back home. Before he could stop himself, he snapped, 'If the fairy Frodite Peree is really a holder of one of the greatest honours in the Hidden World, then I think it's a shame!'

The Gulls had gone deathly white, and Selena and the nymphs looked terrified.

There was a long silence as Pan stared at Thomas, his bright eyes very sharp indeed. Then all at once his face relaxed. He laughed. 'You are well-chosen, Rymer.

The best of your kind are always outspoken and fearless. And you little Middlers have shown more courage than is characteristic of your kind, coming right to beard me in my den! Very well. You shall ask me your question. What is it?'

Thomas stammered, 'Sire . . . we just wanted to know – did you, of your own hands, grant the Order of the Horns of Pan to Frodite Peree the Ariel?'

'I remember no such name,' said Pan, at once. 'But then, it is possible I have met the lady under another name. What is she like?'

'Very pretty,' said Pinch, speaking for the first time.

Pan raised an eyebrow. 'Ah, so you speak too! Pretty, then, eh?'

'Not so *pretty*,' said Patch, sharply. 'More *flashy*, really. Long blonde hair, big blue eyes – you *know*.'

'I *do* know,' Pan said, grinning. 'Well, let me tell you, my friends – she's no Ariel that one, and I'm surprised at you Middlers, getting taken in like that. You must have got soft. Still, I suppose she's a very clever one, it's true. No point goggling at me like that, my friends – you see, she's a witch, a human witch, though there's most definitely Ariel blood in her ancestry somewhere not too far away. Pretty enough, anyway, you're right, boy.' He grinned. 'And bright. *Very* bright. Pity, really.'

'Sire?'

'Pity I had to send her packing, her and that ill-favoured friend of hers, husband, master, whatever he was.' He paused. '*He* was a real Hidden Worlder.'

The children looked at each other. Thomas said, carefully, 'Who was he, Sire?'

'How should I know?' said Pan, shrugging. 'He didn't give me his real name, just called himself the Master. No business of mine what silly name he chose to call himself, he wasn't the one asking for the favour.'

'Did she have any children with her, Sire? Or speak of any?'

'No. She had no children, nor spoke of any. Doesn't mean she didn't have any, though, left behind wherever she came from.'

'Did she say where that was?'

'Oh, somewhere in your world, Rymer. Can't remember the name. It's not important, anyway. Enough to know she was a human.'

'What name did she give, Sire?'

'Lily – I think that's what she said. She *was* like a lily,' he added, dreamily. 'Pretty and perfumed as a lily. She stayed a while, you know . . .'

'Sire – forgive us – but did you grant her the Horns of Pan?'

'No. I did not. Pretty she was, and very clever, and good company for a while, but a bit of a troublemaker. She loved to play tricks on dryads with those little white mice of hers, sending them up people's sleeves, down fauns' burrows, popping up in the most

110

unexpected places . . . well, you know, I love a joke, but a lot of others don't. People complained. It got tiresome. Besides, I've never granted the Horns of Pan to a human, even one with Hidden World blood, and never will. It's simply not done.'

'Why then,' said Patch, cheerfully, 'she's a liar and a fraud, and we can just go back home and tell them that.'

'Won't they be mortified, in Owlchurch, when they find out how they were taken in!' said Pinch, hugging himself in glee.

But Thomas saw the expression on Pan's face. He said, quietly, 'It's not quite so simple, is it, Sire?'

Pan looked rather sheepish. 'You've got me there, Rymer. No, it's not quite so simple. There are certain cases when . . .' He paused. Thomas and the Gulls waited, breathlessly. 'Well, you see,' he went on, hastily, 'once granted, the honour cannot be taken back. And there have been the odd occasions when holders have proven unworthy, and have taken themselves out of the reach of vengeance, far away into the human world. Would such a one pass on her award, out of spite, to an unworthy recipient? It is not impossible.'

Pinch and Patch looked horrified. 'But, Sire! We thought . . .'

'That the system was foolproof, my friends?' Pan's voice was a little tired. 'It used to be. But times have changed. The system works on trust and honour, and if that's gone, well! I cannot police every single detail, you know. I've been ruler here for thousands of years. Have you any idea how many times the Horns of Pan have been granted over that time? No, I'm sure you haven't. But I can tell you it is far too many to keep in mind.'

Thomas said, 'But, Sire – do you think that is what happened? That Frodite Peree found someone willing to give her their own Horns of Pan?' Seeing Pan's expression, he added, 'You *knew* she did?'

Pan looked at him. 'She hinted that her friend – husband – whatever – had told her there was a holder back in her family tree. I didn't ask any more questions.'

'But why not, Sire?'

Pan shrugged. 'What was the point? As I said, times have changed. We used to be able to trust most other Hidden Worlders, even the Uncouthers. Not any more! As to humans – don't get me started. They used to know their place. Not now!'

'But, Sire, if you could only have warned . . .'

'Warned *who*? How was I to know where she and her little friend were going, and why? In any case, I've decided I don't care any longer about the world outside the Syrinx. As long as we Arkadians are left alone to live in our own way, then what does the rest matter?'

There was a long silence. Pan closed his eyes, dismissively. 'I have answered a great many questions. That is enough, now. In any case, nothing can be done about your little problem. It's too late.'

'Oh, but, Sire!' cried Thomas. 'You can't let it happen! You've as good as told us that Frodite Peree, or Lily, or whatever her name is, has obtained her crest by some sort of trickery or treachery, with help from that Master person. If people get to know that, they won't respect Arkadia any more. And no one will care about getting the Horns of Pan!'

Everyone gasped. Pan slowly got to his feet. 'Are you threatening me, boy?' he said, darkly. 'Beware. Have you any idea what I can do to you?'

'I can imagine,' said Thomas, shaking a little, but knowing he had to speak. 'But, Sire, you must see. Arkadia's always been famous for its wonderful magic. Sire, you say times have changed. But I don't think they have. I haven't been in the Hidden World for long, but even I can see that getting the Horns of Pan is still a great honour. Why, in Owlchurch the village is even prepared to turn its back on Old Gal – just because of Frodite Peree and her Horns of Pan!'

'Told you she was a troublemaker,' said Pan, with that dreamy smile again. Thomas felt annoyed. It was obvious the Arkadian king had a very soft spot for that fraud of a Frodite and wasn't prepared to be serious about her doings.

'But, Sire,' he went on, 'people in the Hidden World won't think so well of Arkadia if they realise what's happened! And in the human world, if enchanters and witches find that the Horns of Pan can be forged, then every crook and cheat will do it. What's more, if the news gets out about how the great Pan himself was tricked, people will laugh. Even in my world, people still tell stories about the great lord Pan. But that'll change, too. People will make a joke out of you, Lord Pan!'

'Thunder and lightning!' shrieked Pan, throwing out his arms. At once, the sky turned black, huge bolts of lightning flashed, thunder boomed so loud it made them all jump with fright. 'Fire and flood!' he screamed, and they heard the whoosh of flames and the rush of water. 'Wind and tempest!' he bellowed, into a shrieking gale and a howling storm. He grew tall, taller, so tall he seemed to take up the whole world, his strong arms flinging havoc around him, his handsome goatish face twisted with mad rage. Then suddenly, as quickly as it had started, the noise and wild wind stopped, the sky returned to its normal colour, and Pan stood there looking down at the children. He was not as tall as he had been, but much taller than when they'd first seen him. And the expression on his face was not pleasant to look at.

'Selena, bring me my wax seal, a sheet of parchment, a quill, an envelope. Now!' The girl took off like a scared rabbit, and was back in next to no time, with the items. Pan, who hadn't stopped staring angrily at Thomas, snatched them from her hand, scrawled something on the parchment, put it in the envelope, closed it with the seal.

'You are all three going back to Owlchurch. At once. You will take this letter back with you. This will put things right. And if I hear one snide whisper, one sneering murmur, about Arkadia, anywhere, I will know where to find you, Rymer. I will be watching you. Do you understand?'

'Perfectly, Sire,' said Thomas. He was cold all over, shaking like a leaf, desperate to get out. He had got what he wanted, he thought, but at the cost of making an enemy of Pan. And that was quite a price to pay.

Then he felt Patch's little hand in his, and heard Pinch's quavering, but still determined voice. 'We will be with him, Sire, every step of the way.'

'And much good it might do you,' said Pan, coldly. 'This is a bold and reckless Rymer who will change your little world, Middlers.'

'He already has,' said Patch, softly, and she

squeezed Thomas's hand. 'And we're glad of that, Sire.'

Pan stared at the three of them. Then he turned away. 'Go. Go before I change my mind,' he said, tightly. 'Selena, seeing as you brought them here, you are to escort them to the border.'

'Yes, Sire,' said the girl. She looked scared.

'And do not linger there. I have a good mind to close the borders altogether. It is clear the world outside Arkadia no longer knows the bounds.'

'Sire,' said Thomas, sadly, 'it is not that at all. Please, Sire, don't turn your back on the rest of the world.'

But Pan was not listening. He had turned and was striding away, his flock of nymphs fluttering after him like frightened butterflies after a raging bear.

FOURTEEN

Nobody spoke much on the way back across the river and into the glade. Selena seemed anxious to be rid of them. That wasn't surprising, thought Thomas. He *had* rather burned his bridges with Pan, hadn't he? The Green Man had told him to beware, but he had spoken his mind, anyway. He wasn't sorry he had, not really, for it made him angry to see how little Pan cared, or how lightly he took the whole thing. Well, at least he had Pan's letter. He'd have to make sure Angelica got it. But would she be back, by the time they got back to Owlchurch?

How *would* they get back? The unicorn – oh dear, he'd meant to say something about the unicorn's strange behaviour to Pan – was gone. He had no idea how far Arkadia really was from Owlchurch. But if, say, the unicorn was as fast as a light plane, and you compared that to how fast you could go on foot – why, it might take them days and days! Even weeks. And by then, it would be too late for Old Gal. Not to speak of the fact that his own father would be dead worried about him. His heart sank. Oh, what had he done with his rash words? Why couldn't he have been cleverer, more patient?

They came to the edge of the glade. Selena stopped. 'I have to leave you here,' she said, uncomfortably. She pointed east. 'You came from the direction of the rising sun. It's about to dawn. Just follow that. Goodbye.'

'I'm sorry,' said Thomas, helplessly. 'I didn't mean to be rude to your King.'

'But you were,' said Selena, bleakly.

'I know. I just couldn't bear to hear him brush us off. It's very important to us, and—'

'There's something you should know,' broke

in Selena. 'Something from our country, added to a spell, always magnifies it. It's an interesting fact, don't you think?'

They looked at each other, blankly.

'You heard,' said Selena. She tapped her pocket, said, 'Least thing I can do, thank you for the cards,' and then, with a casual wave, and a cheery 'Bye!' she was off, running away from them across the glade, and out of sight.

'Well!' said Thomas, staring after her. 'What *could* she mean?'

'Oh, True Tom,' scolded Pinch, laughing, 'she was trying to give us a clue, without attracting Pan's anger.'

'How can it help us?'

Both twins shook their heads at him. 'Thomas, you can be very slow,' said Patch, kindly. 'I think we ought to do the long-stalker spell, don't you?' she went on, turning to her brother. He nodded.

'Oh!' Light dawned in Thomas's brain. 'You mean, if we use something from here – like if we stuff our shoes full of Arkadian grass – it'll make that spell stronger, and carry us further?'

'You got it,' said Pinch, grinning.

Thomas grinned back. 'Of course! I thought that before, that maybe something was making my card-tricks work so well. Well, thank goodness for Selena. I thought we were going to be ages walking back.'

'There's one problem,' said Patch. 'The normal long-stalker spell makes you go seven times as fast as you would normally walk. We don't know by how much the spell will grow once we stuff our shoes. Will it double, or triple, or more?'

Pinch and Thomas looked at her, crestfallen. 'And we don't know just how far Owlchurch is from here, do we?' said Thomas.

'No,' said Pinch. 'But a unicorn generally travels a hundred times faster than we can walk. She took about fifteen minutes to dump us at the glade.'

'And that was from your father's house.'

'I think anyway we should go to Father's before we go to Owlchurch,' said Patch. 'He can help us.'

'We don't have time,' said her brother. 'Look at the sky, it's already nearly dawn. We've got to get back with this letter at once. Who knows what Frodite Peree's up to, right now? Besides, if Father hears what happened with Pan, he won't be very happy. Pan might not be what he used to be – what people used to look up to – but *still* . . .'

They stared a little glumly at each other. Thomas said, 'Anyway, we'd better give it a try, and hope for the best. Let's stuff our pockets with grass too and if the lot we put in our shoes is not enough to carry us as far as we want, then we'll still have more to keep revving the spell up!'

'Good idea!' said Pinch and Patch, at once.

Soon, their shoes were stuffed most uncomfortably full, and their pockets bursting too. They held hands in a circle and repeated the words of the long-stalker spell. The shoes began to wriggle and jiggle, then in a rush of wind, they were off, faster than they'd ever gone before, so fast that their feet left the ground and they went soaring up into the air, high above the tops of the trees.

It was wonderful, just like a dream Thomas had once had. They were floating above the trees, able to see a long way. The rising sun's light splashed out over the huge forest, and in the far, far distance, they could just about see streams sparkling, smudges of smoke, tiny dots of houses. When Thomas turned back, once, craning to catch a last sight of Arkadia, he saw nothing but unbroken green tops, nothing to show where the secret forest kingdom lay, with its whimsical, selfish king. I wish . . . he thought, then pushed the wish away. What was done could not be undone. And he didn't regret it, not really.

But it was still a pity. He thought of Selena, of the fauns, the dryads, the nymphs, the centaur. He would have liked to see a little more of Arkadia, and Arkadian magic. Well, now he could forget about all of that. Him, and the Gulls too. For them, it might well be worse. After all, people in the Hidden World even swore by the Horns of Pan, and if Arkadia completely closed its borders as a result of their intrusion, the Gull children would not be popular!

All at once, his shoes gave a kind of sickening judder, and he felt his stomach lurching downwards too. Pinch shouted, 'We're about to run out of fuel! We're going to have to land, very carefully, just into the top of that big tree there. OK? All together now, descend!'

It was not a soft landing. Branches whipped at their faces and limbs; but they managed to break their fall in the leafy canopy, and sat in the topmost branches, catching their breath. After a moment, Patch crawled out to the edge of the limb on which they sat and looked down into the forest below.

'Well?' said her brother.

'Can't see much,' said Patch. 'No idea where we are.'

'I think we're still deep in the forest,' said Thomas. 'We've only been flying for about ten minutes, and we weren't going as fast as the unicorn did.'

Pinch was pulling out the grass in his shoes. 'Look, it's all withered! All the juice has gone out of it. Lucky we thought of taking extra.' He stuffed handfuls of fresh grass in his shoes. 'Come on, let's go!'

They took off again. It didn't seem quite as fast this time. The forest stretched on endlessly beneath them, and the streams and smoke and houses seemed almost as far away as before. The morning was well and truly started now. It might be hours before they arrived.

But only a short time later, the spell began to fail again, this time in a sputtering sort of way, like an engine coughing. Sitting in yet another tree, they pulled out the grass – blackened this time, as if by frost – and pushed in more handfuls.

But it was a much harder take-off this time. The shoes hardly cleared the tops of the trees, and kept jerking and juddering in such an unpleasant way that Thomas began to feel rather ill, and scared too. To make it worse, a little, cold wind had begun to blow, a wind that was steadily gaining in strength and would soon make it difficult for them to steer properly. 'I think we should land, and try and use the spell along the ground,' Thomas shouted, above the noise of the wind. 'I don't think the grass has enough power left to make us fly. The further it gets from Arkadia, the weaker it gets.'

FIFTEEN

He was right. The grass in their shoes was crisp and useless, and the last handful in their pockets was very limp. There were holes in their shoes that hadn't been there before. It was clear that the strengthened power of the spell had been a bit too much for them.

'It probably means the pishogue – the magic – will leak out of them very quickly,' said Patch, bleakly. 'If we're not careful, the long-stalker spell itself won't work at all.'

'It could even be worse,' put in her brother. 'It might even go backwards.'

'You're cheery, both of you,' said Thomas, crossly. 'What choice have we got? Come on, let's put the last handful in.'

It was a rather glum trio who made their way along the forest track. They were going fast, but because it was on the uneven ground, it wasn't half as comfortable as before, more like being in a really bumpy, jerky car with bad suspension. Thomas felt his very bones jarring up and down, and his teeth rattling in his head.

It wasn't long before the shoes began to slow down again. The children stopped briefly, pulled out the useless grass, and gritting their teeth, said the long-stalker spell again. The shoes seemed reluctant to go, but eventually, they kangaroo-hopped into an uncertain start. Up and down the track they went, dragging their unhappy riders with them, bump over a stone, lurch, over a log, ooof, through some undergrowth, going more and more slowly, winding down, down, like an engine slowly dying. 'Go, go, you stupid things!' shrieked Pinch. 'Go, or I'll turn you into beetles and stamp on you!'

At that moment, Patch stopped dead. 'Can you hear it?'

'What?'

'A unicorn! Coming this way! Really fast!'

'Wait!' said Thomas, as both Pinch and Patch instantly scrambled up the nearest tree. 'We can ask her to give us a lift!'

'Don't be a fool!' shouted Pinch. The drumming of hooves was getting very loud. 'Get up here.'

Thomas hesitated a moment too long. He only just had time to dive into the undergrowth when the unicorn burst on to the track, wild-eyed, covered in sweat. It was Silverhair. But she was not alone.

An ominous, masked figure, squat and misshapen, crouched on her back, covered completely in a hooded, dark full-length coat. One gloved hand was holding a rein; the other, a nasty steel-tipped whip, and its feet were in spurred boots. Thomas could not see the face at all. But he shuddered as the figure turned this way and that, obviously looking for someone, or something. He really hoped it was not for them! He pushed back into the undergrowth, very quietly, trying to stop breathing, hoping the Gulls could stay quiet too.

The rider was pulling on the rein, turning the unicorn round and round, the spurs digging into it. Silverhair looked quite crazy with fear; trembling all over, her eyes almost bulging out of her head, her nostrils flaring, her breathing harsh. Thomas thought, it's him, the rider, she's afraid of. Who is it?

Then it came to him. Of course! What a fool he was! This must be the person the Arkadians had described, the one who'd come with Frodite Peree. Unlike Frodite, he was a creature of the Hidden World, some powerful being who called himself the Master. He was in league with the so-called Ariel. And he must be hiding in the forest, somewhere, waiting for . . . waiting for what? For Frodite to completely take over in Owlchurch, so he could move in and . . .

He started. The unicorn was screaming and pawing the ground just under the tree where Pinch and Patch were hiding!

It happened very quickly after that. The rider pulled something out of its coat – something that unrolled like a large net – and, springing off the unicorn's back, darted with monkey-like swiftness up into the tree. Shrieks and yells announced that Pinch and Patch weren't taking it quietly. But in less time than it takes to write it, they had both been thoroughly rolled and wrapped in the net, slung over the Master's back. The creature sprang back on to the unicorn – just as Thomas sprang out of the undergrowth and ran straight at Silverhair, shouting, 'No! No! Silverhair! Don't let him do this to you! Silverhair, you are a free spirit, from a great clan! You don't have to bow to an evil magician's will!'

Silverhair screamed and reared and plunged.

The Master fought to control her, but he was hampered by the burden on his back. Thomas danced around, trying to encourage the unicorn. 'Throw him off!' he yelled. 'Come on, Silverhair, do it for all of your great ancestors! Do it, Silverhair, and your name will be sung throughout the ages!'

The unicorn was fighting back. But the Master was clinging on too, gripping hard, digging his spurred boots cruelly into the creature's flanks, the whip whistling in the air. A pattern of blood sprang up on the silver coat. Poor Pinch and Patch, tumbled together in the net, yelled at the tops of their voices, as did the Master, screaming words Thomas couldn't make out, in the din. There was something oddly familiar about his voice. Yet Thomas was quite sure he'd never seen the Master before, anywhere.

'Come on, Silverhair!' he urged, coming closer, sensing the unicorn was losing heart. 'Come on, you—' But he never finished his

sentence, for just then the Master caught him a stunning blow on the side of the head with a spurred boot. Seeing black and red stars, he crashed helpless to the ground, Pan's letter flying out of his pocket.

The unicorn was beaten now. She was staggering, her flanks covered in blood and sweat, her head lolling. The Master pulled hard on her rein, making her jerk up. He looked down at Thomas, who stumbled. The Master cracked his whip. The stinging steel tip of it bit into Thomas's cheek. Again the whip came down. It snaked around Thomas's feet, making him fall over. The Master bent down, curled the whip around the letter, and picked it up. 'Pan's seal?' he said. 'That'll do nicely! Thank you, Rymer, you've been more useful than you can know! Owlchurch will be ours!' And digging his spurs into the unicorn's flank, he screeched, 'Off we go!'

The unicorn turned, whirled once, then took off down the forest track with its burden,

Pinch and Patch, still yelling, bouncing up and down in the net on the Master's back. In an instant, they had disappeared.

Thomas got gingerly to his feet. Everything hurt. His cheek was bleeding where it had been cut by the whip. His back was aching where he'd fallen so hard. His throat was hoarse from yelling. His head pounded. But worse of all, his heart was gripped with hopelessness and fear. The Master – whoever he was – and Frodite had won. They held all the winning cards now. And it was clear to him that their plans must go way beyond just pushing Old Gal out of the village. They wanted to take it over completely.

He never would have imagined before that could happen. He'd always thought Owlchurch was far too strong and sensible. But what he'd seen recently, when a pretty, clever witch had somehow managed to completely hoodwink most of the Owlchurchers, had made him think twice about that. And his experience in Pan's kingdom hadn't exactly helped, either.

SIXTEEN

Now what was he going to do? He had no proof of Frodite's treachery, and the Master had taken Pinch and Patch. He was a long way from Owlchurch, and even if he managed the long-stalker spell by himself, there was no guarantee it would work properly. His shoes were a mess now, all holes and tatters. The magic would leak out as fast as it rushed in.

For a moment, he just felt like giving up. Then he thought of his friends' faces – they had looked cross and indignant more than scared, as they fought and struggled in the Master's net – and he pulled himself up. Stop being such a wimp, he told himself sternly. You have to try. For their sake, you have to try.

He began to recite the long-stalker spell to himself. As he did so, his shoes began to twitch, and soon they were kangaroo-hopping into action again, bumpily down the forest track. The pace was slower than you could hope for, but at least it was quite a lot faster than normal walking, and Thomas found that if he kept muttering the words of the spell as he went, it kept the shoes moving along at that pace. But the shoes were wearing out fast – he could really feel the stones and twigs of the path.

He had been going along for a little while when suddenly he heard the sound of an engine. It was a high, thin whine, like a mosquito buzz. If this wasn't a Hidden World forest, he thought, he'd have imagined a fast motorbike was coming down the track towards him. As it was . . .

It was better to be safe than sorry. The

Master and Frodite probably had other helpers, and who knew what monstrous form they might take? Thomas plunged off the track, into the undergrowth. The engine noise was getting louder and louder. In the next moment, the thing itself appeared.

Peering from his hiding-place, Thomas saw that it was indeed a motorbike – a smart cream and silver machine of the sit-up-and-beg kind. But it was not that which made Thomas break cover, and run shouting in astonished relief towards the newcomers. For riding on it – splendid in cream and silver leathers, and silver helmet and goggles, her chestnut hair streaming behind her – was none other than the Lady Pandora, from Aspire! Balanced on a little seat behind her, looking very messy indeed beside her neat elegance – none other than Bosky, the Green Man's servant!

Lady Pandora reacted very well to Thomas's sudden appearance. She drew her machine up right at Thomas's feet. Bosky jumped off.

'Knew we'd find you!' he chuckled. 'Where are the Gulls? Boss is waiting for you all.'

Thomas gulped. 'I don't . . .'

Lady Pandora had been watching Thomas. 'Bosky, really,' she drawled, 'can't you see the boy has had a shock? We were too late, weren't we?' she went on, taking off her silver goggles. Her bright green eyes were fixed on Thomas's face. There was an oddly kind expression in them that Thomas had never seen there before. He nodded, silently. 'Then there's no time to waste,' said the Lady Pandora, briskly. 'Get on, Thomas, just behind me. Bosky, you run as fast as you can, back to your boss, and tell him to meet us at the Aspire bridge. But mind, there's to be no smashing of things: this rat has to be caught cleverly, in a trap, not by force. Understand?'

Bosky gave a cold smile, nodded, and took to his heels. In a dream, Thomas got on the bike behind the First Lady of Aspire, and hung on to her waist as she put her goggles back on, turned her machine around, and started it again. Like all Hidden World machines, this motorbike only *looked* and *sounded* like the kind you might see in the human world. It wasn't petrol that drove the engine, but the concentrated power of dream-insects, trapped and furious in the clear fuel tank.

Lady Pandora revved the engine, making the dream-insects whine loudly, and went hurtling back up the track, scattering pebbles and twigs. Despite the speed and the rough track, however, the ride was comfortable and smooth, like riding on a cloud.

Thomas wanted to ask the Lady Pandora a million questions but he knew that the Aspirants liked to be the ones to question people, so he kept quiet.

After a while, she threw over her shoulder, 'Aren't you wondering why I'm here?'

'Well . . .'

'Of course you are. Humans are always nosy,

especially Rymers. Well, then. Old Gal came to see us, straight after Frodite Peree appeared in the village.'

'*Old Gal?*' So that was where she'd been when she took off, he thought. He'd never have thought she'd go *there* for help!

'What's the matter, Thomas? Think we wouldn't speak to her? What a fool you are. She may be of a lower standing – and her marriage was altogether ill thought and selfish – but we *know* her. We do not know this stranger, this creature who has stolen Owlchurch's heart. It seemed to Mr Tamblin and me that there was something altogether dodgy about her, and her story. It seemed to us that this could be trouble, Real trouble, and not just for Owlchurch, but more importantly, for *us*.'

Thomas remembered what Hinkypunk had said, about Frodite Peree's settling in the village being 'one in the eye for the Aspirants'. He couldn't restrain a grin as he thought that jealousy might well have pushed the Aspirants into taking action.

'When Old Gal described the crest to us, in perfect detail, Mr Tamblin and I understood at once that the so-called holder of the Horns of Pan was a fraud. You see she claimed to have *just* been granted the award. But *that* design went out many years ago. Mr Tamblin and I keep up with Arkadian fashion and it was clear from Old Gal's description this one was right out of date. The shade of green was wrong, for a start, and there should have been two small twists and one bigger twist to the horns, not three twists exactly the same. It then seemed clear to us that she had stolen it or borrowed it from someone who'd been granted the award long ago.'

Thomas listened in astonishment. He'd never have thought knowing about fashion could be so useful! Lady Pandora seemed to feel his amazement, for she said, in an amused tone, 'Of course, no one in Owlchurch pays any attention to what's new, so they wouldn't have known. And besides, the only one who might possibly have worked it out – Angelica – was away. As to Morph, he's a good dream-maker, but hopelessly old-fashioned, and he never goes out of the village. Owlchurch sets so much store on the old things, the old ways, that they've really been caught in a trap this time. Between you and me, Thomas, Arkadia isn't quite what it used to be, I hear.'

'I know,' said Thomas, quietly.

'Yes. I suppose you do.'

'Lady Pandora? How did you know to come and find us?'

'I didn't. What happened was we had planned to meet Old Gal again last night, but she never came to the meeting-place. We went to her house and she was gone, and so were her children. We slipped into the village and found you were gone, too, Thomas. Well, we decided you must all have gone into the forest, to meet the Green Man and ask for his help.'

'You did?'

'The Green Man is an outlaw. He ranges widely. He might well know something, you see. Anyway, Mr Tamblin stayed on watch on the hill near the Gulls' cottage, and I went to find the Green Man. He told me what had happened. And I realised firstly that Old Gal was not with you; and secondly, that you three children might well be in danger. We have been getting strange reports of disturbances in the woods, lately – of rogue unicorns and the like – you see.'

'Oh,' said Thomas. Why couldn't they have told Owlchurch about these reports? he thought. Why did they always have to keep things to themselves so much? Still, he had no right to complain, not after what Lady Pandora had done. He said, hastily, 'Thank you for helping me. I don't know where Old Gal is, but Pinch and Patch have been captured by the accomplice of Frodite Peree – or rather, Lily, that's her real name – he's a creature called the Master. He's from the Hidden World, but she's not.'

'What!' The Lady Pandora brought the bike to a skidding stop. She twisted around and pushed up her goggles. Her green eyes were fierce. 'What do you mean?'

'Er . . .' Thomas smiled weakly. 'Pan told me – Frodite Peree – she's not an Ariel, though apparently she does have Ariel blood. She's a human witch, and her name's Lily.'

'Lily what?'

'Don't know. Pan didn't seem to know.'

She snorted. 'Hmph! Mind you, if she has Ariel blood from somewhere, that might explain the crest – her ancestor maybe held it, long ago. Maybe she was somehow unworthy, and either was thrown out and took herself out of the Hidden World. Yes. That's possible.'

'That's what Pan said. And her accomplice, he's the Master, he's a strange, crooked-looking thing, all wrapped up in a big hooded coat, and a mask, and gloves, and boots – all covered, you see.'

'Then he'll either be an Uncouther or a Montaynard, a mountain-man,' said Lady Pandora, at once. 'They don't like the sun of the Middler lands very much.' She frowned. 'But why would any of these seek to stir up mischief right now?'

'Pan didn't say . . .' Thomas trailed off. A sudden memory had jumped into his mind. He thought of the Master's voice. Could it be that . . . ?

'Lady Pandora, is there any way that an Uncouther would leave Pandemonium by himself and come up into our country?'

She stared at him. 'As spies, yes, on the orders of their rulers. It's been known. But then you would never see them, and they wouldn't stay long. Uncouthers are mob creatures, by nature, otherwise. Oh, they come as traders, when we have a Magician's Convention – but only in groups, and strictly supervised.'

'But would they ever do it – for themselves, not on the orders of their Queen, or the General?'

'Unheard of!'

'Unheard of, but not impossible?'

'I've never heard of it,' said Lady Pandora, starting off down the track again. 'No, that Master of yours *must* be a Montaynard. Though why on earth . . . ? We have good relations with them, generally, though they are cross-patched and take offence very easily. What interests me more is the witch, Lily.' Grimly, she added, 'She has made a mockery of all our attempts to regulate human magic. I have warned Owlchurch many times to work with us on a modern Register of Approved Witches and Enchanters. They still operate on the old system, with great big books and quill entries. Our dream-maker Fantasos – who as you know is Morph's brother – has devised a wonderful new system for us, completely foolproof, updated every week. It also has an appendix of banned magicians. No doubt Lily would be on that.'

'But perhaps she's never tried this trick before, Lady Pandora.'

'Perhaps she hasn't. And perhaps she has. She was rather slick about it, wasn't she? As if she'd had a lot of practice. No, I would say she's done this before, in other places, and there'll be a file on her.'

'What about her children, Lady Pandora?'

'You're full of questions, aren't you? I don't think they're of much importance, really. Just local colour for her. She's magicked them up, I expect. A kind of match for Old Gal and her twins, you see. And judging by their looks – why, *who* wouldn't want a family like the Perees rather than the Gulls as ornaments to their village?'

'I wouldn't!' said Thomas, fiercely.

Lady Pandora laughed her musical laugh. 'I know *you* wouldn't, Thomas dear. And in this case, despite the Gulls' unfortunate past, and their tendency to look like untidy birds' nests, I daresay you are right. Looks do not always make the man, or the woman.'

From the exquisite Lady Pandora, that was quite some admission.

SEVENTEEN

They soon drew up at the edge of the forest. Instead of looking down over Owlchurch, though, they had come in on the Aspire side of the River Riddle. Lady Pandora turned off the engine, sending the dream-insects to sleep. The bike rolled silently down the hill towards the glittering village, with its tall crystal tower sparkling in the bright air. Down in the high street of Aspire, Mr Tamblin, joint Mayor of the village with Lady Pandora, was waiting for them. He was in his usual smart black, his long black hair slickly tied back, but there was a slight anxiety on his face that Thomas had never seen before, not even when they'd been in Pandemonium trying to outwit General Legion Morningstar.*

'There you are, Pandora. Thomas. Where are the Gulls?'

'Explain later,' said the Lady Pandora. 'What's up?'

'Big trouble across the river,' said Mr Tamblin. A slight, superior smile curled his lip. 'I always thought it might come to this.'

'Stop that,' said the Lady Pandora, sharply and surprisingly. 'No time for I-told-you-so's.' She can talk! thought Thomas, amused despite himself. 'What's happened?' she added.

'This morning, at dawn, Frodite Peree declared herself new Mayor of the village. She's installed herself in Morph Onery's Dream Emporium. She was able to take it over because she had some accomplice, hidden in one of Morph's messy store-rooms . . .'

'The Master!' said Thomas and Lady Pandora, together.

* A tale told in *Thomas Trew and the Hidden People*.

'The what?'

They explained, quickly. He nodded. 'I see. Should have known. Well, anyway, she's declared that a new, mischief-making line of dreams will be her first mission as Mayor. She and her friend, they're keeping lots of people hostage in the Emporium – your father, Thomas, Morph Onery, and that bookseller fellow, amongst others. In fact I think most of the village is there.'

'Most? Did anyone escape?'

'Oh, Hinkypunk did. But he's powerless to do anything much. She's called up a magic fog around the Emporium. It's very strong magic, stronger than anything we've seen in a while. In fact I suspect she's drained all the pishogue out of Owlchurch to make it. Well! She might have got her Horns of Pan by fraud, but she certainly deserves them for the power of her magic!'

'It sounds like you admire her,' said Lady Pandora, shortly.

'Well, why not? Never seen anything like it. Girl's running rings around everyone. Even you, Pandora dear. She's got to be something pretty special, you must admit.'

Pandora's face looked like thunder. 'Nonsense! She's just a witch, a human witch with Ariel blood. Some renegade, no doubt, who crossed the border and married a human. And she's in league with a Hidden Worlder, anyway. Maybe she does have talent, but so what? She's a troublemaker, and not only in Owlchurch either, you mark my words!'

'True enough,' said Mr Tamblin, with that slight smile again.

Thomas couldn't stand it any longer. 'Sir, I know she is plotting with the Master to take over the whole of the Middler lands! Including Aspire! She plans to rule Owlchurch – but her accomplice will rule here, in your place!'

He'd made all that up, of course. He didn't know anything like that. But he did know it would make Mr Tamblin take notice. The

Aspirant reddened with anger. 'What! How dare they even think . . . Who could have the hide to . . .'

Thomas looked steadily at him. 'Sir, I think the Master is actually an Uncouther come to take revenge on us all for what happened in Pandemonium.'

Both Mr Tamblin and Lady Pandora stared at him. 'You think General Legion Morningstar . . .' began Lady Pandora, carefully.

Thomas shook his head. 'I can't really say who I suspect. I'd rather not say the name out loud, just yet. You know what Uncouthers are like about names.'

Mr Tamblin looked thoughtful. 'Hmm. Yes. You can have power over an Uncouther with his name, if you startle him with it at the right time.'

'Yes. Anyway, maybe this Uncouther . . . maybe he brooded on what we'd done, and decided to take revenge on us all. Maybe it's him, working with the witch Lily, right now.

Maybe he even got her the Horns of Pan in the first place, or at least told her how she could get them.'

'That's a lot of maybes,' said Mr Tamblin. He grinned, slowly, baring sharp teeth. 'But *maybe* you're right.'

'I know he's got my friends, anyway. And the witch has got my father, and the others. This isn't just about being unfair to Old Gal, now. We've got to defeat them – *both* of them, sir – for everyone's sake.'

'You don't need to teach me my duty, boy,' huffed Mr Tamblin. Lady Pandora gave a slight, mocking smile. Mr Tamblin tossed his head. 'Well, it's high time to get down to the bridge and see if the Green Man's turned up. Or am I the only one interested?' And he turned and strode away, his perfect hair like a great thin stream of black water on his straight black-suited back.

'You go on down there with him, Thomas,' said Lady Pandora. 'I'm going to check

Fantasos' file, see if that Lily witch is mentioned. Knowing about her past history could come in useful.'

'But what if she's not . . .' Thomas began, but he was speaking to himself. Lady Pandora was already gone.

When Thomas got to the bridge, Hinkypunk was there, talking with his opposite number in Aspire, Monsieur Renard, as well as Mr Tamblin. There was no sign of the Green Man, yet.

Hinkypunk detached himself from the others, and came towards Thomas. He showed no surprise at seeing him. 'There you are, True Tom. Things a bit exciting, hmm?'

'Pretty scary,' said Thomas.

Hinkypunk showed all his sharp teeth in a smile. 'Scary? Don't believe you, boy.' He lowered his voice. 'Now then, you remember the yallery?'

Thomas started. The yallery, a nasty little

creature which repeated everything you said till you nearly went mad, had been bred in Hinkypunk's shop. The trickster werefox took it with him when he went with the others to rescue Thomas in Pandemonium, and he had left it there as a present for the General.

'I can see you've been thinking along the same lines as me,' said the werefox now, winking at Thomas's expression. 'Best keep quiet about it, you're right, till we're sure.' He paused, then went on, 'You really put the cat among the pigeons, vanishing like that, you four. Forced their hand, you did, I think. Should have lain low a bit longer. I could see she was fishy from the get go; somewhat of an actress, in fact. But you should have waited.'

Thomas shrugged, annoyed by Hinkypunk's words. 'Yes, and *you* should have said you thought she *was* fishy! We could have used your help. We couldn't wait. Besides, *she* wasn't going to wait. She always meant to do this before Angelica came back, you know that.'

Mr Tamblin and Monsieur Reynard were strolling towards them. Hinkypunk drawled, 'Maybe; but what have you really gained from your rash actions, True Tom?'

Thomas glared at him. 'I think I know who the so-called Master is. And that she's no Ariel, but a human called Lily . . .'

'And how's knowing that going to help you now?'

'You'll see,' said Thomas, tightly. But he spoke to shut Hinkypunk up. He didn't really *see* what he could do at all, at least not about the witch.

'Slight change of plan,' said Mr Tamblin, reaching them. 'Hinkypunk, Monsieur Reynard thinks you and he might be able to cook up some creature that might somehow be able to slide into that fog of hers.'

Hinkypunk looked cynical, but he nodded. Monsieur Reynard said in his soft, prim voice, 'I think you'll be pleasantly surprised by my facilities, dear colleague.' The Owlchurch trickster's red eyebrows rose nearly into his hair then, and he gave a mocking little smile.

'No doubt I'll be overawed, Reynard, my friend,' he drawled. 'Lead on, then. Let's see what nonsense we can cook up together, eh?'

As they left, he winked at Thomas. Annoying creature! thought Thomas. It was all very well for Hinkypunk to be cool and cynical, but he'd done nothing to expose Frodite Peree or help Old Gal, when he could. Typical. He was still fuming when Mr Tamblin said, quietly, 'Here he comes, that shambling old thing. By the horns of Pan, I shouldn't think he's changed his outfit in two hundred years!'

The Green Man was coming out of the woods, Acorn and Bosky and Skrob by his side. It was like seeing a tall tree, surrounded by three stumpy bushes, suddenly up roots and start marching across the countryside. Tall and angry tree; stumpy and angry bushes, and waving something about . . .

'Oh, dear oh dear, they've brought clubs,' sighed Mr Tamblin. 'I told them we're not doing any of that smash and grab stuff! Just imagine, that's what they did all those years ago in Morph's Emporium. He'll be hopping mad if he sees them – might even add his spells to the witch's to keep them out, and we'll have a real situation on our hands. I'll have to head them off. Wait a moment, Thomas.'

And he was off, running up the slope towards the Green Man and his gang. Thomas was left staring after him.

EIGHTEEN

Left alone, Thomas hung around uncertainly. Something inside him was telling him that whatever the Aspirants were planning, it might not work. The witch and the Master had outsmarted everyone. And yet, something else was nagging at him – some dim idea shaping down in the bottom of his brain. It was something to do with something Hinkypunk had said, something that had set off a red flag in Thomas's mind. But what was it? Suddenly, he gave an exclamation, as that *something* became clearer in his mind. Could it be that . . . Could it really be?

He jumped up on to the bridge. He could see the Aspire gate-keeper watching him in astonishment as he puffed red-faced up to her.

'Bridge is closed,' she said in her sweet voice as he came up to her. 'Orders of Mr Tamblin and Lady Pandora.'

'You've got to let me through,' he said. 'Come on.'

'Orders,' said the girl, stubbornly. Thomas looked at her a moment, jumped up on to the parapet of the bridge, and before she could stop him, he'd leapt into the River Riddle with a big splash. He could hear shouts up on the hill and knew that Mr Tamblin and the Green Man must have seen him, but he couldn't worry about that.

The river was deep and swift, and the current swept him away downstream. But maybe the Riddle wanted to help him, for it washed him right to the spot on the bank where he and the Gull twins usually sat.

He scrambled out of the river and ran up the hill to the cottage. The door was open, but no one was there. Where was Old Gal? Perhaps she'd already been captured by the Master?

He ran out again and down the hill towards the village. He glanced up and down the street. It looked terrible. All the shops, including the café, were dark and deserted, doors open and banging on their hinges. Saint Tylluan's church seemed to have lost a corner of the owl-ears shaped tower that gave the village its name. And Morph's Dream Emporium was invisible, replaced by a huge bank of what looked like big fat black fog, or cloud. A nasty cold wind was blowing up and down the street, and all the trees had lost their leaves, which had all turned black and brown, and blew down the street, along with a hollow, dirty old pumpkin shell. Not a soul was to be seen.

Thomas's heart sank. He thought of what Mr Tamblin had said, about suspecting that the witch had drained all the pishogue out of Owlchurch to make her magic protection. She must have done it with help from the

Uncouther. Maybe together the two of them were too powerful to fight against just now? Maybe Thomas would just have to beg them to let the prisoners go, and just leave Owlchurch to them? But then he looked again at the once-cheerful little village, where he'd spent so many happy days. Wild anger surged through him. How – *why* did they do this? Why hadn't those two strangers stayed at home and left Owlchurch alone?

He raced up the steps into the Apple Tree Café. He went into the front room. There was dust and grime and spiders' webs on everything, as if it had been deserted for years. He took the stairs two by two. The rooms upstairs were just as empty, and just as dirty. There was nothing and no one there at all.

And then, he was at the doorway of his room, about to turn tail and go downstairs again, when he heard a noise. A little noise. A squeaking noise, somewhere in there. Whirling around, he slammed the door with himself in the room. He peered around.

It was dark and empty in the room; all the furniture, including his marvellous dream-travel bed, was gone. But just there, down under the window, crouching in shadow – a flash of something white! It moved; but Thomas moved too. The white thing squeaked, and wriggled, but Thomas held on tight to it. Then he saw another white thing flash by his foot, and he was about to come down on it, when a squeaky voice spoke, 'Please, don't do that!'

Thomas started. The voice said, 'Please – we don't mean any harm.'

Thomas looked down at his hand. A little white mouse crouched there, trembling. It had mild blue eyes, eyes that were familiar and that looked pleadingly at Thomas. He said, 'Who are you?' though he already had an inkling of the truth.

'I'm Squeak,' said the mouse.

'And I'm Squeal, at your feet,' said a shy

voice on the floor. Thomas looked at the mouse in his hand, then the one at his feet. *'You were her children,'* he said, slowly.

'She turned us into human things!' said Squeak, indignantly. 'Imagine that, how horrid, to go from nice soft fur to horrid bare skin. And the spell was so strong it made us dumb. We couldn't even utter one word!'

Thomas remembered how the Peree twins had seemed unable to speak. He even remembered what he'd said to them: 'Cat got your tongue?' He couldn't help smiling at the memory. No wonder they had reacted so badly!

'Why are you smiling?' said Squeak, suspiciously.

'Nothing,' said Thomas, hastily. 'That is . . . Pan told me she had two white mice pets always with her. I should have guessed.'

'Pets!' said Squeak, crossly. 'We're from an important family in our country, I'll have you know.'

'Where's that?'

'In the Kingdom of Mus, second mouse-hole under the stairs in her house,' said Squeak promptly. 'She promised that if we came with her, we would see the world, and make our fortune!'

'But now she has no more use for us,' said Squeal, sadly.

'She's dumped us,' said Squeak. 'And because she's taken all the magic from this place, we're back to being mice. That's why, too, her carriage and horses – which were really a pumpkin and two beetles – have vanished. She cannot spare any more magic for us, thank goodness.'

'But now we're stuck here. We can't go home,' whispered Squeal. 'And I do so want to go home. Mother and Father must be so worried.'

'Right,' said Thomas, thoughtfully. 'What do you think of the witch now?' he asked.

'Think of *her*! We *hate* her! She's treated us like . . . like common dirt!' said Squeak, drawing his tiny self up. 'She lied to us!'

'And that creature with her . . . that thing from the underworld . . . he frightened us. He treated us cruelly,' whispered Squeal.

'Would you help me, then? Help me defeat them both?'

'Help you? Well . . .'

'What do you want more than anything?'

'To go home,' said Squeal.

'I promise we'll get you there, if you help me now.'

'Very well,' said Squeal, before Squeak could speak. 'What do you want us to do? Is it . . . is it dangerous? We're only little, and . . .'

'It's not dangerous, don't worry. It's quite simple really,' soothed Thomas, hastily. 'I just need you to tell me something.' And he bent down to both little creatures, and asked them a question. When he'd finished, they looked at each other. Then they both began to speak, at once. Thomas listened. 'I thought so,' he said, when they'd finished.

'What are you going to do, then, Thomas?' said Squeak.

'Put an end to all this,' said Thomas. 'It's high time.'

'Can we come with you?' whispered Squeal. 'We'd love to see what happens.'

'If you like,' smiled Thomas. 'If you don't think you'll be scared.'

'Of course we won't be scared!' huffed Squeak. 'Why, we—'

His sister cut him off. 'Can we hide in your sleeve?' she asked, shyly. 'Promise we won't tickle.'

'OK. If you like,' said Thomas.

NINETEEN

Outside, the village was colder and darker than ever. The big black foggy cloud that hid Morph's Emporium from sight seemed thicker and larger. But it wasn't that which made Thomas's heart beat faster. It was a strange underground thump, right under his feet; a rumble that was like the beating of a distant drum.

He lifted his arm up and spoke to the mice clinging on to his sleeve. 'Oh no! It's the Uncouthers. They're on the march!'

'Don't worry, Thomas,' said a voice behind him. He turned. It was the Green Man, with his friends, and Mr Tamblin. 'It's not too late.' And he marched straight up to the cloud,

spread his arms – and suddenly, from out of his hands, long snaky vines sprouted, thick and strong. His legs thickened, his neck bulged with cords, a creaking, groaning sound came from all of his muscles as he started to shed his human shape and become more and more like a giant tree. Meanwhile, Bosky, Acorn and Skrob had lined up next to him. They were changing shape too, long thorns and sharp prickles breaking out all over them, so that very quickly they looked more like giant hedgehogs than anything else.

'Forward, men!' came the Green Man's voice. It had changed too – it was a deep, roaring sound, full of a huge, inhuman force, as if the forest itself was speaking.

The Green Man and his friends walked right into the cloud. There was a rending, tearing sound. Vines and thorns snaked up and down the face of the cloud, making a kind of vicious plant-web. Then a branch stabbed up and through the cloud. There was another rending sound – and part of the web fell away, with part of the magic cloud wrapped in it, like a cocoon. It was like the tearing away of a curtain. Thomas could see a little further into the fog now; could just about see the faint outline of the Dream Emporium.

'They've got through the first layer. Well! It's good to have the power of the forest on your side, I must say. Wait here; I'm going in to help them,' said Mr Tamblin, and he walked into the fog, vanishing at once. But Thomas wasn't going to be left behind.

'Squeak and Squeal, I'm going too. You'd better stay here. It's too dangerous for little creatures like you.'

'No,' said the mice, faintly but firmly. 'It's too dangerous *out here*, with all that sticky fog-magic rolling around, and those branches and vines and thorns flying about!'

Walking into the fog was like being thinned, only worse. Thomas couldn't see anything, but he was surrounded by horrible, clammy, gluey air, that clung to his skin, as if long, creepy fingers were trying to drag him under. Where the vines had touched it, it also had a horrid smell to it, like something rotting in a compost heap. Thomas felt sick. He could feel panic rising in him in great scary waves, but he fought it down. It made him feel even sicker. But he kept going, blindly. He had to reach the Emporium!

But it's never easy to find your way in a fog, especially a magic one. Thomas had been walking for a while before he realised he was going round and round in circles. In his sleeve, the mice were very quiet, though he could feel them trembling. Then suddenly, he heard that underground thump again, and this time it was much louder. Bang, bang, bang, just under his feet. And then, all at once, the ground opened; a big crack groaned wide, and Thomas only just stopped himself from falling. A sulphurous smell came from the crack, and an angry voice shouted, 'Fustian Jargon! I summon you back! I summon you back! Disobey at your peril!'

It was a voice Thomas recognised at once. The voice of Queen Lilith, formidable ruler of Pandemonium and mother of General Legion Morningstar! But before he could ask himself any questions, suddenly, out of the fog, appeared a hooded, masked figure, wrapped entirely in a black coat: the Master! It was crawling reluctantly towards the crack, as if compelled by some force much stronger than itself. As it reached Thomas, it looked up; the hood fell back, and Thomas saw the head of the Uncouther, an odd cross between a tortoise and a monkey. It was indeed Fustian Jargon, who had been the General's right-hand man, until the coming of the yallery, brought by the Owlchurchers when they had come to rescue Thomas.

For half a second, Fustian glared at him. His eyes had an angry red light in them. He growled, 'I lost my job, my position at court because of you and your friends. I was the butt of jokes from one end of Pandemonium to the other! I wanted revenge!'

'Fustian Jargon,' came the Queen's sharp voice, 'I summoned you, and I don't want to wait. I will count to three . . . *One!*'

'I'm clever. I've done what no Uncouther has done before me. You haven't heard the last of me, all of you,' snarled Fustian Jargon. 'You haven't, you wait and see!'

'It was your General's fault, not ours,' said Thomas, shrugging. He felt nothing but contempt for the Uncouther. 'You should blame him.'

'*Two!*'

'Anyway, it's too late!' shrieked Fustian Jargon, edging towards the crack, his face twisted with fury. 'Your Owlchurch is gone, anyway! Dead! Gone! *She'll* rule over you! Ha!'

'*Three!*' said Queen Lilith, and Fustian disappeared into the crack like a jack back into his box. In the next instant, Thomas gasped in complete surprise, for from out of the narrowing crack suddenly jumped a thin, dishevelled figure, rather the worse for wear – the last figure he ever expected to see.

Old Gal shook herself, looked at Thomas, raised an eyebrow, and said, 'Had to go and ask her help, no other way, knew the witch must have had help from somewhere there, against the rules, yes.' And she loped rapidly into the fog, vanishing from sight. At the same moment, the crack snapped shut with an almighty crash, like a pair of metal jaws closing. The crash shook the ground, then slowly, the echoes died away.

Around Thomas, the fog seemed to be thinning away too. But it still clung to his face, his arms, his hair. And it smelt worse than ever. Yet he could see further now; could see he was only a few short steps away from the front door of the Emporium. And he could see Mr Tamblin there, looking through the windows. He turned when he heard Thomas. 'Oh, it's you.'

'Did you see . . . did you hear . . . ?' gasped Thomas. Mr Tamblin's face was rather pale, and there were beads of sweat on his impeccable brow, but he said as coolly as ever, 'You mean the Uncouther Queen taking away her servant? Yes. A good thing, eh? And about time.'

'That was Old Gal's doing,' said Thomas. 'Old Gal, do you hear?'

'It would seem so,' said the Mayor of Aspire, raising an elegant eyebrow. 'Cleverer than we thought, what?'

'No,' said Thomas. 'I always thought she was. Clever. Brave. Everyone's taken her for granted. They can't, now.'

'Er,' said Mr Tamblin, 'it's not over, you know. The Uncouther's gone – good riddance. Well done, Old Gal. But there's the witch, Lily. She's still holding all those people. And she's too clever for any of them. At the very least, we'll have to give her what she wants.'

'Ha! I don't think so!' said Thomas, sharply. And he pushed open the door of Morph's Emporium, and walked in.

TWENTY

And there she was, Frodite Peree, or the witch Lily, or whatever you wanted to call her, sitting like a beloved queen on a high-backed chair, her devoted people at her feet. Except that everyone looked very miserable indeed. There was quite a crowd. Amongst them was Morph, shrunk into himself, his face grey with shame; there was Monotype, his usually bright smile turned to a scowl; there was Thomas's Dad, with a bewildered expression on his face. All of them were very still, as if . . .

'As if they've been turned to stone,' said Frodite Peree, sweetly, smiling at Thomas. 'It's not quite like that, dear Rymer. It's just I'm holding them trapped in a moment of time.'

Thomas wasn't looking at her. His eyes searched the room for Pinch and Patch. But they weren't there.

'What have you done with them?' he said.

'What are you talking about, Thomas? Listen to me. I've decided that I need someone to help me rule. I need a clever person. I need you!' She leant forward earnestly to him. 'You know how good I am, don't you, Thomas? You heard what they've all been saying.'

'Stop it!,' said Thomas, through stiff lips. 'You're beaten. That Uncouther who helped you, he's gone. He won't come back. You can't do anything without him, you needed his magic to make your tricks work here. It's over.'

She shook her head, smiling. 'Don't be silly. You and me, Thomas – we could rule this place. We're both human and from the Hidden World; we're much better than both combined. We've proved that, you and I. Come on, Thomas! What do you say?'

'I say Pan was right not to grant you the Horns of Pan,' said Thomas, looking at her for the first time. 'You *could* only get such a thing through trickery.'

The witch's porcelain skin reddened with an ugly blush. 'It was not trickery! It was my right! I inherited it from my great-great-grandmother! By what right did they exile her, just because she married someone they didn't approve of?'

Thomas stared at her. She laughed bitterly. 'Yes! That's right! Just like Old Gal! Fustian told me all about it. But *my* great-great-grandmother didn't have an Angelica Eyebright to protect her! She was cast out! Just like that! She had to make her way in our world the best she could.' Her face twisted. 'What right did Pan have to deny me the right to bear her crest, just because I'm from the human world? Why should things be like that? Thomas, haven't you thought how unfair it all is?'

He did not reply. He hadn't expected any of this. He must do what he'd planned to do, but it was harder than he thought. He could almost feel sorry for her. After all, it was true that all that stuff was really unfair.

'Thomas!' squeaked an urgent voice, close to his ear. 'Remember what she's done. Remember how she uses people. Don't trust her!'

'What's that?' said Frodite Peree, sharply. 'Who spoke?' A not-very-nice smile began to steal over her face. She got up, slowly. 'My dear little mousekins, is it you? Come here to mummy, little mouse-child, come here to me! Come on, the three of you. Come on, dear Thomas, dear mouse-children . . .'

Her eyes were fixed on Thomas. They were glowing with a strange, deep light, and he could feel himself being urged forward, wanting to put himself into her hands, to trust her, to believe everything those lovely eyes said. But he'd seen it before. He was safe! And now he found the strength in him to shout,

'The show's over, Lily Lafay! Yes, I know who you are – I remember seeing you on TV, back in London, in that show.'

The witch's face was very still, but shock had leapt into her eyes. 'What *are* you talking about?'

'I know who you are! You're an actress – you're in a show called *Spellbound High*, about a school of young witches and wizards! You had a small part in it, I remember. You were one of the teachers – and in the story, you were called Madame Aphrodite Parry. Frodite Peree!'

'You're raving,' said Lily, but she was white to the lips. 'Look at me, Thomas. Look at me!'

'No,' said Thomas. 'This is the best act you've ever put on, you'd win prizes for it in any talent show anywhere in all the worlds, but we've seen through all your tricks, you see. Your Uncouther friend's gone. The curtain's coming down!' And he began to clap, softly at first, then more and more loudly, till his palms ached. And all at once, all around him, the stiff, frozen figures began to move, to stretch, to say, 'What? What happened? Where . . . ?' and then there came a hammering at the door, and Mr Tamblin came rushing in, followed by Hinkypunk and the Lady Pandora. Then came the Green Man, who creaked and groaned as he came in but who had returned to a more human shape and size. And then Thomas heard his friends' voices, shouting for him, and the voice of their mother, telling them off for running too fast. And he shouted, 'Pinch and Patch!' and ploughed a way through the crowd, leaving the bewildered Lily standing there.

Pinch and Patch were none the worse for wear, and shouted to Thomas about how it had all felt, and how their mother had rescued them, and how the unicorn had snapped out of her bewitchment the moment Fustian Jargon vanished. But then they felt a great silence at their back, and turned to see all the Owlchurchers, and the Aspirants, and the forest men, and the mouse children, all standing in a menacing circle around the witch Lily. She was shrunk now, her hands held out helplessly in front of her. All the shreds of glamour and magic that had clung to her had gone. She was an ordinary fair-haired young woman, quite pretty but not astoundingly beautiful, and scared. *Definitely* scared.

'You are a wicked creature. You have broken all our laws,' said Morph, harshly.

'Stolen our trust,' said Monotype, heavily.

'Tricked a lot of people,' said Mr Tamblin, raising an eyebrow.

'Been a complete and utter troublemaker,' snapped the Lady Pandora.

'Sown chaos,' said Old Gal, sharply.

'You must be punished,' said the Green Man.

'Severely,' grinned Hinkypunk.

'Yes!' squeaked the mouse-children. More voices added to the cacophony, till the room was a babble of excited, angry sound.

'Wait,' said Thomas. He walked over to Lily.

'Wait. You all said how good she was, before.'

'And how bad!' said the Lady Pandora, sternly.

'Yes. But the fact is, she outsmarted everyone, didn't she? She proved that sometimes a good dose of human magic – of that strange magic we call acting – combined with some Hidden World gifts, can actually outperform anything else, in all the worlds. Think of that.'

'We do,' growled Morph Onery. 'She's dangerous!'

'She's unapproved,' said the Lady Pandora. 'I checked! There's no mention of her in the Register, not even of banned witches. She's not like you, Rymer. She's not known to us as a regular border-crosser. She slipped between the cracks, illegally. That's why she must be . . .'

'Employed, I should think,' said Thomas, calmly. 'Employed to check up on everyone else. You should put her in charge of the combined Owlchurch and Aspire Register of Approved Enchanters and Witches, make sure no crooks get in.'

There was a long silence. Everyone stared at Thomas, especially Lily, who looked at him as if she'd never seen him before. Then Hinkypunk began to laugh. 'Set a thief to catch a thief?' he gurgled. 'I like it! I like it!'

'A combined Register?' said the Lady Pandora. She shrugged. 'Well, I suppose it could be done. If Owlchurch will bother to get its mess of papers in order, that is.'

'How can you say that?' said Morph Onery, furiously. 'We know exactly what we . . .' He trailed off, as everyone looked at him. 'Well, anyway,' he huffed, 'it could easily be done, if Angelica agrees.'

'I think she will,' said Thomas.

'And I'm *sure* I will,' said Angelica's voice. Everyone fell back as she walked in through the door. The Mayor of Owlchurch was covered in dust and she looked exhausted. But

190

she was smiling. 'I don't think Adverse has ever driven so fast,' she said. 'Yet it seems we were almost too late.' She looked at Thomas and the Gulls. 'I think we can all say we're very lucky to have you here. And very grateful, indeed.'

They all flushed, and shifted their feet. Angelica smiled, and continued, 'Your idea is good, Thomas. At least about the combined Register, and maybe even about *her*.' She turned to Lily, and her face changed. 'But she can't just get away with what she's done. She must, indeed, be punished, and quite severely. I suggest we set her to clean up Owlchurch thoroughly. Scrub it from top to bottom. And run errands and gather ingredients for Old Gal.'

Pinch and Patch fell about laughing. Thomas grinned.

'You weren't an ointment-maker at all, girl, were you?' said Angelica to Lily. 'Your speciality was glamour; making people believe things you wanted them to believe. That's an

Ariel gift.' Lily nodded, meekly. 'Well, girl, you certainly did that. You've made a lot of people look very silly indeed. You allied yourself with an Uncouther. You told lies and spread chaos wherever you went. Do you think your punishment is too severe?'

'I . . .' Lily began, hotly, then bit down on her lip. 'I didn't mean it to get quite so serious,' she whispered, after a moment. 'But Fustian Jargon said . . .' She gulped. 'I'm sorry. I really am. I'll do anything you want me to do, especially . . . especially . . .' She turned impulsively to Old Gal. 'I really am sorry. I do so admire you . . . truly . . . I . . . I was envious . . . I did so want to work with you . . .'

'And so you shall,' said Old Gal, sharply. 'There's lots of washing-up to do, my girl, I can tell you.'

Gales of laughter followed this speech. But Angelica said, 'I don't think this girl is the *only* one who should apologise to Old Gal and her family, do you, my friends?'

Throats were cleared, feet shuffled. Uncertain, ragged voices mumbled apologies. Morph especially looked very sheepish indeed.

Lily said, softly, 'I'll do anything, if you'll only consider letting me stay, afterwards. You see, it's all I've ever wanted. All I've ever dreamed of, being in the midst of magic . . . real magic, not just shadows on the screen. I'm so sorry I made such a mess, and that I was so mean and selfish. It all . . . sort of ran away with me, in a way. It all went to my head.'

Gareth Trew spoke for the first time. His voice was quiet and grave. 'I think *we* were to blame, too,' he said, turning to Angelica. 'I think we should remember that. We were prepared to believe everything she said. Because we . . .' His eyes slid to Lily's face, and then away. 'Because we *wanted* to,' he went on, very softly indeed.

Poor Dad, thought Thomas. He really, *really*

liked her. His eyes met Lily's. She looked down at her feet. She looked utterly miserable.

Angelica had been watching. Now she said, briskly, 'We'll see. We'll see. Pay your debt, Miss Lily Lafay, and we'll see.' Her stern face relaxed a little. 'It's true enough, what Gareth said. And I suppose you did us a favour, really. You showed us our weaknesses.'

The crowd looked very sheepish then, especially Morph, Monotype and Thomas's dad. But the Aspirants looked as superior as ever. Thomas could just guess what they were thinking. *They* hadn't been taken in. They hadn't been tricked! Ha, he thought, a little sourly, that lot will never change!

'There's one more thing,' said Angelica. She beckoned. Old Gal came forward, rather reluctantly. Angelica beamed at her. 'I think that in a day or two, I shall be making a trip to Arkadia. And I—'

Thomas, breaking in, said, 'I don't think Pan will be very welcoming.' Quickly, he explained what had happened. But before he'd finished, Lily took something out of her pocket and silently handed it to Angelica. Thomas recognised it at once. It was Pan's letter!

With everyone watching, Angelica broke open the seal, and read the letter. She shook her head, slowly. 'He says that he was wrong in taking things lightly; that the girl Lily has not been granted the Horns of Pan, though her ancestor had a right to it. He also says, Thomas, that you are a rare Rymer, and that Owlchurch is fortunate in both you and the Gull children. That is all. Nothing harsh or unwelcoming there, I would have thought.'

Thomas's heart filled with astonished gladness. He thought, how strange and unexpected people can be! And then he thought, why, that means . . . that means . . .

Angelica was still talking. 'My dear friend,' she said, to Old Gal, 'I will go to Arkadia – with you, and your children, and Thomas. And as Mayor of Owlchurch, I will be asking King

Pan, in the strongest possible terms, to grant you his highest honour – the Horns of Pan. It will be more than deserved, and greatly overdue.'

There was silence. Everyone stared at Old Gal who stood as if stricken dumb. Then the Green Man said, heartily, 'And so say all of us!' His cry was taken up by Bosky, and Acorn, and Skrob, and Pinch, and Patch, and Thomas, and then Monotype, and Hinkypunk, and Gareth, and then the rest of the village, and even the Aspirants, who clapped politely. Only Morph said nothing for a moment or two; then seeing everyone was looking crossly at him, he grunted, rather reluctantly at first, then more lively, 'And so say I, so say I, too!'

Old Gal looked at them all as if she couldn't believe her eyes. As the cries died away, she dabbed at one eye, fidgeted nervously, muttered, 'So much fuss, so much fuss!' Then she turned to Angelica, and for the first time ever, Thomas saw Old Gal break into a

smile, a real smile. 'Don't mind if I do,' she
said, calmly.

The cheers nearly lifted the rafters, then.
And Thomas and the Gull twins cheered
louder than all the rest.

Thomas Trew and the Hidden People

Sophie Masson

Thomas feels different from other people. He sees things no one else sees. He hears things no one else hears. He feels as if he's waiting for something to happen.

Then one day it does. A truly extraordinary person appears in his home.

A dwarf.

And this is only the beginning . . .